RIVER OF EARTH

JAMES STILL

River of Earth

with a Foreword by Dean Cadle

The University Press of Kentucky

For My Mother and Father

Cover illustration by Barbara McCord
Cover design by Jonathan Greene

Publication of this volume was made possible in part
by a grant from the National Endowment for the Humanities.

Scholarly publisher for the Commonwealth,
serving Bellarmine College, Berea College, Centre
College of Kentucky, Eastern Kentucky University,
The Filson Club Historical Society, Georgetown College,
Kentucky Historical Society, Kentucky State University,
Morehead State University, Murray State University,
Northern Kentucky University, Transylvania University,
University of Kentucky, University of Louisville,
and Western Kentucky University.

Editorial and Sales Offices: The University Press of Kentucky
663 South Limestone Street, Lexington, Kentucky 40508-4008

ISBN 0-8131-1372-5

Library of Congress Catalog Card Number: 77-92928

This book is printed on acid-free recycled paper meeting
the requirements of the American National Standard
for Permanence of Paper for Printed Library Materials.

Manufactured in the United States of America

FOREWORD

JAMES STILL completed *River of Earth* in an ancient log house on a small eastern Kentucky farm, green and flowering, between Wolfpen Creek and Deadmare Branch in Knott County, where he continues to live and write, at ease among a valley of neighbors who often sound as though they have stepped out of his stories.

A descendant of pioneers who settled early in the southern mountains, Still grew up in the Appalachian foothills of northern Alabama. When he moved to eastern Kentucky in 1932, the machine age in the hills was less than thirty years old; and of the millions of people whose lives it had affected perhaps no one, even the coal-mine owners, sincerely believed it was a blessing.

For two hundred years the people of southern Appalachia had been independent and relatively self-sufficient. Each family obtained from the land it owned practically everything needed to feed, clothe, and shelter its members. But within a period of less than twenty years this agricultural society of small farms was virtually destroyed by industrialism. Families sold their farms, or abandoned them, or lost them to mine operators, and flocked to the mushrooming mining camps: three-roomed "shotgun" houses, a commissary, a school, and a church, all of whitewashed board and batten, clustered near a driftmouth.

At the height of the coal boom—around 1920—a farmer who seldom had owned a dollar bill could earn from $20 to $50 a day and buy more from the com-

missary in one week than he could grow on a farm in a
year. Then, in the late 1920s the demand for coal de-
creased. Some mines closed permanently, and those that
continued to operate worked from one to three days a
week at reduced wages, and then usually only during
the spring and summer months to stock coal for the
winter demands, forcing the few men who owned land
to choose planting and harvesting or digging coal.

The result was a landless, jobless, hungry, perplexed
people. Ruined for a way of life they could control, they
were betrayed by this new, quicksilver promise that left
them idle much of the year.

The sureness with which James Still weaves his patch-
work of light, shadow, and colors into this drab, joyless
landscape surely creates one of the presences of artistry
that we can recognize and appreciate in all the arts but
cannot isolate and define. Marjorie Kinnan Rawlings
had this quality in mind when she referred to Still's work
as "vital, beautiful, heart-breaking, and heart-warmingly
funny," as did poet Delmore Schwartz who called *River
of Earth* "a symphony," and the *Time* reviewer who
considered it "a work of art."

Still's "secret" lies in his ability to use language so that
it performs the functions of both music and painters'
pigments. Whether the individual words are strange or
familiar, it is the manner of expression that gives them
conviction and demonstrates that Still is a creator as well
as a listener, and that he sees and hears with the senses
of a poet.

His words can create a picture filled with the bril-
liance of an impressionist painting:

Morning was bright and rain-fresh. The sharp sunlight fell slantwise upon the worn limestone earth of the hills, and our house squatted weathered and dark on the bald slope. Yellow-bellied sapsuckers drilled their oblong holes in the black birch by the house, now leafing from tight-curled buds.

And a sound: "January was a bell in Lean Neck Valley. The ring of an ax was a mile wide, and all passage over the spewed-up earth was lifted on frosty air and sounded against fields of ice."

His scenes can be filled with factual knowledge, as in the account of the father removing a cob from a calf's throat. And he can give an idiomatic translation of the Old Testament that retains the rhythm and power of the original, as in Brother Mobberly's sermon:

I was borned in a ridgepocket. . . . I never seed the sun-ball withouten heisting my chin. My eyes were sot upon the hills from the beginning. Till I come on the Word in this good Book, I used to think a mountain was the standingest object in the sight o' God. Hit says here they go skipping and hopping like sheep, a-rising and a-falling. These hills are jist dirt waves, washing through eternity. My brethren, they hain't a valley so low but what hit'll rise again. They hain't a hill standing so proud but hit'll sink to the low ground o' sorrow. Oh, my children, where air we going on this mighty river of earth, a-borning, begetting, and a-dying—the living and the dead riding the waters? Where air it sweeping us?

Published within a year of each other by the same publisher, *River of Earth* and *The Grapes of Wrath* are the only books chronicling the demoralizing Depression years that have continued to gain readers in more affluent ones. The major difference between them is that Steinbeck's story deals with a calamity that has struck America only once in its lifetime, while Still is writing of the struggles that have plagued the mountain people since the country was settled.

Although the Joads travel halfway across the country and the Baldridge family moves only the few miles separating the coal camps from the farm, both books are equally an odyssey of a people in search of a promised land. With the coming of each spring and each fall Brack Baldridge announces that the mines are going to open soon—this time for good. And the mother's continual refrain is: "Forever moving yon and back, setting down nowhere for good and all, searching for God knows what. . . . Where air we expecting to draw up to?"

And when the mines close and the crops fail there is little complaining. They simply pack up and move again, accepting, hoping, laughing to make their misfortune bearable.

More than twenty years before the region was labeled a "poverty pocket" and prior to the surprised reactions of experts and government officials to the problems of destitution, as though they had encountered some recent wonder, James Still had presented the heartbreaking account of what it means for a human being to live out his life hungry and cold. His is not a socioeconomist's collection of figures, causes, and possible cures, but the dramatized plight of human beings accepting poverty without accusations or judgments or rantings against outside institutions.

That fiction for Still obviously is a scenic art is evident in the visual clarity with which he creates scenes and develops characters and in the deceptive ease with which he keeps the author out of the story. Most any section of the novel reads like a mini-play that could be transferred to the stage with a minimum of directives, for the narrative is continually pushed forward by credible action and by dialogue designed more for hearing than for silent reading. And though the reader may insistently remind himself that the story was set down on paper by James Still, he will have to search for overt signs of the author's presence. It would be ridiculous for a playwright to circulate on stage giving cues and interrupting the action to inform the audience of the thoughts of the actors, Still seems to be saying, so why should I muddy the story for the reader by intruding my directives, commentaries, and evaluations? Using the first person point of view of a young boy as his "center of consciousness," Still has achieved a fine balance between erasing the author and creating the impression that the story moves of its own volition. And however far in the background he may be, he is there in the form of a magician busy with one hand entertaining the audience with anecdotes, echoes of folklore, and mountain dialogue while with the other hand he is unobtrusively shaping incidents, bridging-in poetic interludes, and disguising signs that direct the story toward his intended climax.

Still is a writer of constricted lives, valid desperations,

and victories that seem small reward for all the patience and hurt they exact; but in his most successful scenes he creates a world whose resonances echo beyond the last word to the fullness of the reader's capacity to understand. His work reflects a compassion, insight, and objectivity remindful of Katherine Anne Porter ("The Jilting of Granny Weatherall," "The Downward Path to Wisdom") and of Bernard Malamud ("The Loan," "The Magic Barrel").

With each "discovery" and each exploitation of Appalachia, *River of Earth* assumes new meaning and increasing significance both as a chronicle of change and as a work of art. Read today with the strip-mined region as a map—the scalped hills and gashed mountainsides, the ruined farmlands, the dead streams, the flash waters the earth can't contain—even the title assumes a prophecy of doom undreamed of by Brother Mobberly.

An emotional response is the one quality above all for which Still works. There are no games, no literary or historical allusions, no puns, no symbolism, sentimentality, didacticism, or redundancy. He gives no motives, airs no theories, states no beliefs. He simply sets down the experiences of a few human beings during a season of change in a certain place. And he does it in a manner that is simple and unposed and with the perception and restraint that denote an imagination as honest, as controlled, as the needle of a compass. And the emotion is present as certainly as the leaf is in the bud. In giving order to "a handful of chaos" Still has created a new and fresh view of a range of mountains seventy million years old and of a people that promise to survive all industrial upheavals.

I

THE mines on Little Carr closed in March. Winter had been mild, the snows scant and frost-thin upon the ground. Robins stayed the season through, and sapsuckers came early to drill the black birch beside our house. Though Father had worked in the mines, we did not live in the camps. He owned the scrap of land our house stood upon, a garden patch, and the black birch that was the only tree on all the barren slope above Blackjack. There were three of us children running barefoot over the puncheon floors, and since the year's beginning Mother carried a fourth balanced on one hip as she worked over the rusty stove in the shedroom. There were eight in the family to cook for. Two of Father's cousins, Harl and Tibb Logan, came with the closing of the mines and did not go away.

"It's all we can do to keep bread in the children's mouths," Mother told Father. "Even if they are your blood kin, we can't feed them much longer." Mother knew the strings of shucky beans dried in the fall would not last until a new garden could be raised. A half-dozen soup bones and some meat rinds were left in the smokehouse; skippers had got into a pork shoulder during the unnaturally warm December, and it had to be thrown away. Mother ate just enough for the baby, picking at her food and chewing it in little bites. Father ate sparingly, cleaning his plate of every crumb. His face was almost as thin as Mother's. Harl and Tibb fed well, and grumblingly, upon beans and corn pone. They kicked each other under the table, carrying on a secret joke from day to day, and grimacing at us as they ate. We were pained, and felt foolish because we could not join in their laughter. "You'll have to ask them to go," Mother told Father. "These lazy louts are taking food out of the baby's mouth. What we have won't last forever." Father did not speak for a long time; then he said simply: "I can't turn my kin out." He would say no more. Mother began to feed us between meals, putting less on the table. They would chuckle without saying anything. Sometimes one of them would make a clucking noise in his throat, but none of us laughed, not even Euly. We would look at Father, his chin drooped over his shirt collar, his eyes lowered. And Fletch's face would be as grave as Father's. Only the baby's face would become bird-eyed and bright.

When Uncle Samp, Father's great-uncle, came for a couple of days and stayed on after the week-end was over, Mother spoke sternly to Father. Father became angry and stamped his foot on the floor. "As long as we've got a crust, it'll never be said I turned my folks from my door," he said. We children were frightened. We had never seen Father storm like this, or heard him raise his voice at Mother. Father was so angry he took his rifle-gun and went off into the woods for the day, bringing in four squirrels for supper. He had barked them, firing at the tree trunk beside the animals' heads, and bringing them down without a wound.

Uncle Samp was a large man. His skin was soft and white, with small pink veins webbing his cheeks and nose. There were no powder burns on his face and hands, and no coal dust ground into the heavy wrinkles of his neck. He had a thin gray mustache, over a hand-span in length, wrapped like a loose cord around his ears. He vowed it had not been trimmed in thirty years. It put a spell on us all, Father's cousins included. We looked at the mustache and felt an itching uneasiness. That night at the table Harl and Tibb ate squirrels' breasts and laughed, winking at each other as they brushed up brown gravy on pieces of corn pone. Uncle Samp told us what this good eating put him in mind of, and he bellowed, his laughter coming deep out of him. The rio lamp trembled on the table. We laughed, watching his face redden with every gust, watching the mustache hang miraculously over his ears. Suddenly my brother Fletch began to cry over his plate. His shins had been kicked under the table. Mother's face paled, her eyes becoming hard and dark. She gave the baby to Father and took Fletch into another room. We ate quietly during the rest of the meal, Father looking sternly down the table.

After supper Mother and Father took a lamp and went out to the smokehouse. We followed, finding them bent over the meat box. Father dug into the salt with a plow blade, Mother holding the light above him. He uncovered three curled rinds of pork. We stayed in the smokehouse a long time, feeling contented and together. The room was large, and we jumped around like savages and swung head-down from the rafters.

Father crawled around on his hands and knees with the baby on his back. Mother sat on a sack of black walnuts and watched us. "Hit's the first time we've been alone in two months," she said. "If we lived in here, there wouldn't be room for anybody else. And it would be healthier than that leaky shack we stay in." Father kept crawling with the baby, kicking up his feet like a spoiled nag. Fletch hurt his leg again. He gritted his teeth and showed us the purple spot where he had been kicked. Father rubbed the bruise and made it feel better. "Their hearts are black as Satan," Mother said. "I'd rather live in this smoke-house than stay down there with them. A big house draws kinfolks like a horse draws nitflies."

It was late when we went to the house. The sky was overcast and starless. During the night, rain came suddenly, draining through the rotten shingles. Father got up in the dark and pushed the beds about. He bumped against a footboard and wakened me. I heard Uncle Samp snoring in the next room; and low and indistinct through the sound of water on the roof came the quiver of laughter. Harl and Tibb were awake in the next room. They were mightily tickled about something. They laughed in long, choking spasms. The sound came to me as though afar off, and I reckon they had their heads under the covers so as not to waken Uncle Samp. I listened and wondered how it was possible to laugh with all the dark and rain.

Morning was bright and rain-fresh. The sharp sun-light fell slantwise upon the worn limestone earth of the hills, and our house squatted weathered and dark on the bald slope. Yellow-bellied sapsuckers drilled their oblong holes in the black birch by the house, now leafing from tight-curled buds. Fletch and I had

climbed into the tree before breakfast, and when
Mother called us in we were hungry for our boiled
wheat.

We were alone at the table, Harl and Tibb having
left at daylight for Blackjack. They had left without their breakfast, and this haste seemed strange to
Mother. "This is the first meal they've missed," she
said.

Uncle Samp slept on in the next room, his head
buried under a quilt to keep the light out of his face.
Mother fed the baby at her breast, standing by Father
at the table. We ate our wheat without sugar, and
when we had finished, Mother said to Father: "We
have enough bran for three more pans of bread. If the
children eat it by themselves, it might last a week. It
won't last us all more than three meals. Your kin will
have to go today."

Father put his spoon down with a clatter. "My folks
eat when we eat," he said, "and as long as we eat." The
corners of his mouth were drawn tight into his face.
His eyes burned, but there was no anger in them. "I'll
get some meal at the store," he said.

Mother leaned against the wall, clutching the baby.
Her voice was like ice. "They won't let you have it
on credit. You've tried before. We've got to live small.
We've got to start over again, hand to mouth, the way

we began." She laid her hand upon the air, marking the words with nervous fingers. "We've got to tie ourselves up in such a knot nobody else can get in." Father got his hat and stalked to the door. "We've got to do hit today," she called. But Father was gone, out of the house and over the hill toward Blackjack.

Mother put the baby in the empty wood box while she washed dishes. Euly helped her, clearing the table and setting out a bowl of boiled wheat for Uncle Samp. I went outside with Fletch, and we were driving the sapsuckers from the birch when Uncle Samp shouted in the house. His voice crashed through the wall, pouring between the seamy timbers in raw blasts of anger. Fletch was up in the tree, near the tiptop, so I ran ahead of him into the shedroom. Mother stood in the middle of the floor listening. Baby Green jumped up and down in the wood box. Euly ran behind the stove.

I ran into the room where Uncle Samp was and saw him stride from the looking glass to the bed. His mouth was slack. A low growl flowed out of him. He stopped when he saw me, drawing himself up in his wrath. Then I saw his face, and I was frightened. I was suddenly paralyzed with fear. His face was fiery, the red web of veins straining in his flesh, and his mustache, which had been cut off within an inch of his lips, sticking out like two small gray horns. He rushed upon me, caught me up in his arms, and flung me against the wall. I fell upon the floor, breathless, not uttering a sound. Mother was beside me in a moment, her hands weak and palsied as she lifted me.

I was only frightened, and not hurt. Mother cried a little, making a dry sniffling sound through her nose; then she got up and walked outside and around the house. Uncle Samp was not in sight. She came back and gave Fletch the key to the smokehouse. "We're going to move up there," she said. "Go unlock the door." I helped Euly carry the baby out in the wood box. We set him on the shady side of the woodpile. We began to move the furniture, putting the smaller things in the smokehouse, but leaving the chairs, beds, and tables on the ground halfway between. The stove was heaviest of all, and still hot. The rusty legs broke off on one side, and the other two bent under it. We managed to slide it into the yard. Mother carried the clock and the rio lamp to the smokehouse. The clock rattled with four pennies Fletch kept inside it.

After everything had been taken out we waited in the backyard while Mother went around the house again, looking off the hill. Uncle Samp was nowhere in sight, and neither Harl nor Tibb could be seen. Then she went inside alone. She stayed a long time. We could hear her moving across the floor. When she came out and closed the door there was a haze of smoke behind her, blue and smelling of burnt wood.

In a moment we saw the flames through the back window. The rooms were lighted up, and fire ran up the walls, eating into the old timbers. It climbed to the ceiling, burst through the roof, and ate the rotten shingles like leaves. Fletch and I watched the sapsuckers fly in noisy haste from the black birch, and he began to cry hoarsely as the young leaves wilted and hung limp from scorched twigs. The birch trunk steamed in the heat.

When the flames were highest, leaping through the charred rafters, a gun fired repeatedly in the valley. Someone there had noticed the smoke and was arousing the folk along Little Carr Creek. When they arrived, the walls had fallen in, and Mother stood among the scattered furnishings, her face calm and triumphant.

WE lived that spring in the smokehouse, sleeping in two beds pushed close into the corners, and with strings of peppers and onions hanging from the rafters overhead. We planted our garden early, using the seeds Mother had hoarded, but it was long before the vegetables were ready for eating. Mother cooked under a shed Father built against the house. There was no abundance of food and we ate all that was set before us, with never a crumb left. Father told us the mines were closed in the headwaters of the Kentucky River and there was hunger in the camps. We believed that we fared well, and did not complain.

Father's face was thin as a saw blade. It seemed he had grown taller, towering over us. His muscles were bunched on his arms, blue-veined and not soft-cushioned now with flesh. He went hunting, searching through the sedge coves and swampy hollows, never wasting a shot. We ate squirrel and rabbit, broiled over hot coals, for there was not a smidgen of grease left in the stone jar. A handful of bullets was kept in a leather pouch. Never more than three were taken for the rifle-gun, and Father rarely missed.

With spring upon the hills, it was strange to go out

and kill in the new-budded wood. The squirrels moved sluggishly, carrying their young. Rabbits huddled in the sedge clumps, swollen and stupid. Once Father brought a rusty-eared rabbit home, setting Euly to clean it. When she came on four little ones in its warm belly, she cried out in fear of what she had done, flung the bloody knife into the dirt, and ran away into the low pasture. She stayed there all day crying in the stubble, and never ate wild meat again.

We had come through to spring, but Mother was the leanest of us all, and the baby cried in the night when there was no milk. Mother ate a little more now than the rest of us, for the baby's sake, eating as though for shame while we were not there to see, fearing we might not understand, that we might think her taking more than her share.

The garden grew as by a miracle, and the blackberry winter passed with the early April winds, doing no harm. Beans broke their waxen leaves out of hoe-turned furrows, bearing the husk of seeds with them. Sweet corn unfurled tight young blades from weed mold, timid to night chill, growing slowly and darkly. Crows hung on blue air, surveying the patch, but the garden was too near the house. Our shouts and swift running through the tended ground kept them frightened and filled with wonder.

Before the garden was ready, Mother and Euly gathered a mess of plantain and speckled jack and we had salet greens cooked with meat rind. The beans were still young and tender, and the potatoes thin-skinned and small. We watched the beans grow, measuring them day by day with joints of our fingers, and dug under the potato stalks carefully with our hands so as not to bruise the watery roots. We picked off the potato bugs and scraped their egg patches from the leaves. Fletch saved the bugs in a fruit jar, pinching buds to feed them when we were not looking.

We went out into the garden in the cool of the evening, turning the vines to look for beetles on the underleaves. Father would pull a bean and break it impatiently between his fingers, looking hungry enough to eat it raw. "I figure they're fair ready for biling," he would say. "Time we had a mess."

"They hain't nigh ready," Mother would say. "When a bean snaps like you'd broke a stick, hit's time. Wait till they've had their full growth."

One morning we found the heaped trail of a mole across the garden, damp with new earth. Father was angry, stamping the ridge of its path with his feet, packing the ground hard where it went among the bean vines. He whittled two green walnut sprouts, shaved the bark until they were brown with sap, and drove them in the farther ends of the trail.

"That walnut juice ought to git in its eyes and turn it back," Father said, laughing a little savagely, and rubbing his hands in the dirt.

Euly begged Father to dig the mole out. "If'n I had me a moleskin, I'd make a powder rag out o' it," she said. "When I get me some face powder, I'd have a mole rag to rub it on with."

Father looked darkly at her, and she ran out of the garden, ashamed of her vain-wishing.

On the day the men came from Blackjack, Mother was washing clothes, and Father swung the battling stick for her on a chestnut stump. Euly saw the men first as they climbed the hill from Little Carr Creek, and she ran to tell us. "They's three men a-coming, and they got mine caps setting on their heads, and two of them have got pokes."

We went around the smokehouse and looked down. The men were still a quarter mile off, their legs awkward like a hound's against the steep climb. Mother went back to the tubs. Father waited, shading his eyes from the sun-ball, trying to see who they were. And he knew them long before they turned over the last short curl of the path, and he knew why they had come.

"Hit's Fruit Corbitt, and Ab Stevall and Sid Pindler," Father said. "Fruit used to be storekeeper before the mine closed."

The men came into the yard, looking at the gray pile of ashes and charred ends of rafters where our house had burned.

"We heered about your burning," Fruit said. "A puore pity with times so hard, and all the mines closed up tight as a jug. We'd a-come and raised you a house, but we heered you was living in the smokehouse and getting along peart."

"We're so packed-up inside we do all our setting out here on the ground," Father said. "We got one chair, but it's holding a washtub."

"Aye, God," Fruit said. "We've done so much setting these last eight months it's like pulling eye-teeth climbing that hill."

"Setting and hearing our bellies growl," Sid said, dragging the poke he held back and forth across the ground. "The grace o' God tuck us through the winter. We've come out skin and bone. We would a-planted gardens if they'd been any seeds. They were et up. Anyhow, there hain't a place fitten in the camp with all the beasts scratching and digging."

The men glanced toward the garden, now thick with

growing, and with the furrow ridges lost among leaves. Father slouched down, looking worried.

"We were thinking you could spare us a mess o' beans out o' your patch," Fruit said. "Our women-folk and children are right mealy in the face. The company store is empty as last year's bird nest."

"Begging comes hard for us who's used to working for our bread," Ab said.

"The beans hain't half-growed yet," Father explained. "They hain't nigh filled out."

"We hain't asking you to give us nothing," Fruit said, the wrinkles around his eyes webbing. "You'll be paid when the mines open. Aye, God, we're asking for no handout. Our folks need some green victuals."

"They hain't nigh ready," Father said again, and he trod up and down in his tracks without moving from where he stood. Then he looked away, saying quietly and sadly: "I got my first hungry ones to turn down. I never yet turned a body down. . . . Go and see what you can find fitten to eat."

The men walked toward the garden. Mother was hanging clothes behind the smokehouse and saw them jump over the split-paling fence, their pokes flaring in the wind. Father went around to the washtub, standing there helpless, not knowing what to say. Mother began to cry silently, saying nothing.

"You can't turn down folks who are starving," Father said at last, and he knew his words sounded foolish and with no weight. He began to hang a tubful of clothes on the line, spreading them out clumsily until it sagged, and the shirt sleeves were barely clear of the ground. He tightened the line, drawing the raveled cord with all his strength.

The men came out of the garden after a spell. They came with their pokes bulging at one end. We knew they had picked every bean, that not one was left.

"Our womenfolks will be right proud to taste a mess o' green victuals," Fruit said. "You'll shorely get your pay when the mines open."

Sid held up his poke and laughed. "You've got a right fair garden," he said. "I seed a brash o' blossoms on them vines. In a leetle time you'll have all you kin eat."

They had turned to go when Ab suddenly pulled something out of his pocket and threw it upon the grass. It was a dead mole.

"I dug this varmint out o' the garden patch," he said. "I seed where he'd holed under a pile o' dirt and I scratched him out. They hain't nothing can tear up a garden like a mole varmint. You ought to plant a leetle dogtick around. Hit's the best mole-bane I ever heered tell of."

Ab hurried down the hill to catch the others, the rocks rattling under his feet. Euly grabbed the mole and was gone with it before Father could stop her, running swiftly around the house. And Mother ran too, swinging her arms in dismay, for she had heard the clothesline break, and the clean garments now lay miserably in the dirt.

I WAS seven on the twenty-first of May, and I remember thinking that the hills to the east of Little Carr Creek had also grown and stretched their ridge shoulders, and that the beechwood crowding their slopes grew down to a living heart. Mother told me I was seven as we ate breakfast. Father looked at me gravely, saying he didn't think I was more than six. Mother said I was seven for sure. Fletch looked into his bowl of boiled wheat, for he was only five and stubborn. Euly laughed, a pale nervous laughter edged with a taunt. She was going on thirteen and impatient with our childishness.

I knew then it was good to be seven, but I did not know how to think of it. Mother held the baby up and he looked at me, making an odd cluck with his tongue sucked back in his throat. And I thought that if I could know what the baby was thinking, I would know what a large thing it was to come upon another year.

After breakfast I went into the young growth of stickweeds beyond the house, believing my whole life was balanced on this day, and how different it must be from any other. I walked into the creek bottom.

Bloodroot blossomed under the oaks and I sat down there, giving no thought to picking the blossoms as Euly would have done, knowing they would droop at the touch. Sitting there I thought that I would grow up into such a man as Grandpa Middleton had been before he got killed, learning to read and write, and to draw up deeds for land; and I would learn to plow, and have acres of my own. Never would I be a miner digging a darksome hole.

Being so full of this thought I could not sit still. I went on around the hill where wild strawberry plants edged into an old pasture no longer used, for we had no stock and the rails were tumbled and rotting. I ran through a budding stubble, feeling the warm tickling on the soles of my feet. Euly and the birds had been in the strawberry patch already. Bare tracks were there on the grassless spots and the fruit was pecked and torn. A few berries were left, half-green and turning. Euly had been there, saying to Mother there might be enough for a pie, but she had gobbled them all down.

I sat on the rail fence. Blackbirds called their hoarse *tchack, tchack, tchack.* Young crickets drummed their legs in the grass—young, I knew, for their sounds were thin and tuneless.

Suddenly there was laughter, long and thin and near. I searched the weed-filled gullies, looking at length into a poplar rising full-bodied and tall at the lower end of the pasture. Euly was swinging in the topmost bough. Fear for her choked me. I called to her to come down, half envious of her courage, but more afraid than anything. She laughed, swinging faster and holding out one hand dangerously.

Fletch was over the hill. He heard us shouting and came up the slope, hurrying on his short legs. His hands were clutched against his pockets.

I ran to meet him, and Euly came down out of the tree to see what Fletch had. He reached one hand into a pocket to show us. It came out filled with partridge eggs, broken and running between his fingers. Euly's face became as white as sycamore bark. She began to cry, knotting her fists and shaking them about. Then she opened one hand swiftly, slapping Fletch on the cheek, and was gone in a moment, running silently as a fox over the hill.

Fletch squalled until he was hoarse, the eggs and tears mixing on his face. I had to find him a pocketful of rabbit pills to get him to stop.

On the day I was seven Clabe Brannon came for Father. His mare was in labor, and he had come wanting help, bringing an extra nag for Father to ride. Father was handy with stock and knew a lot of cures.

He knew what to do for blind staggers, the studs, and bloats. He knew how to help a mare along when her time came.

Fletch and I had just come from the strawberry patch when Clabe rode up. Father came out of the garden, where he had been hoeing sweet corn. Clabe was in a hurry and would not get down, but Mother fetched him a pitcher of cool spring water. Father got on the nag and the stirrups were too short. His legs stuck out like broomsticks. Mother laughed at him.

"Biggest load's on top," she said. "You'd better give that nag a resting spell before long."

"Size don't allus speak for strength." Father grinned. "This here nag could carry me twice over and never sap her nerve."

Father looked down at me, standing there laughing with Mother. "Think I'll fotch this little dirty mouth along for ballast," he said. He reached down, pulling me into the saddle behind him, and I went up over the hind quarters limp with surprise, for Father had never taken me along before. We rode off down the hill, but I did not look back for all my joy, knowing that Fletch's face was shriveled with jealousy, and knowing that I was seven and this thing was as it should be.

We went along up Little Carr Creek, the nag nervous with our unaccustomed weight, her flesh shivering at the touch of Father's heels, and her hips working under me like enormous elbows. Her hind feet bedded in sand and Father clucked. She jumped, almost sliding me off. Clabe took the lead at the creekturn, reining his mount back and forth across the thin water, keeping on firm ground. He rode far ahead.

We were soon beyond any place I knew and white bodies of sycamores stood above the willows. The hills were a waste of fallen timbers. Sprouting switches grew from the stumps, and the sweet smell of a bubby bush came down out of the scrub.

"That there is Stob Miller's messing," Father said. "He's got a way o' leaving as much timber as he takes out. A puore fool would know white oak is wormy growing on the south side of the hill and mixed with laurel and ivy."

And we went on. I counted four redbirds flying low in sumac bushes, and there was a wood thrush repeating its uneasy *pit pit* somewhere. Around more turns there were patches of young corn high on the hills in new-grubbed dirt. Chickens cackled up in the hollows. Sometimes I could see a house set back in a cove, and even when I couldn't see for the apple trees and plum thickets, I knew people lived there by the homeplace sounds coming down to the creek. I knew a big rooster walked in the yard, and there were hound dogs under the puncheon floors and stock hanging their heads over the lot fence.

"They's liable to be a colt a-coming over at Clabe's place," Father said. "How would you like to have a leetle side-pacing filly growing up to ride on?"

"If'n I had me one I'd give nigh everything," I said, "but I'd want it to be a man-colt."

"Clabe might not want to get shet o' him though," Father said. "I reckon he wouldn't want to promise off a colt before he was weaned."

"Reckon I could get that colt?" I asked, my heart pounding, and knowing suddenly there was nothing I wanted more than this. To have a colt, living and breathing, was more than being seven years old; it was more than anything.

"There ain't no sense trying to see afar off," Father warned. "It's better to keep your eyeballs on things nigh, and let the rest come according to law and prophecy."

We crossed the shallow waters of the creek, back and forth to firm sandbars. Silver-bellied perch fled before the nag's steps, streaking into the shallows under the bank. Father looked down at them, laughing at their hurry.

"Skin your eyes and see the fishes," he said.

Clabe's wife came out on the porch to meet us, her spool legs thrust down into a pair of brogans. Two children hid under the porch, looking out with dirty faces, and an old hen, bare of feathers behind the wings, pecked in the yard. Guineas stretched their long necks through the fence palings.

"You was a spell a-coming," Clabe's wife said. "A wonder the mare didn't bust before you got here."

We went around the house to the barn. The hip-roof was broken and sagging. Oates, Clabe's boy, waited for us in the lot, watching the mare. He was older than I, taller by a half-foot, and he had buck teeth. Two of them stuck down in the corners of his mouth like tushes. He grinned at us and I thought, looking hard at him, that he had a face pine-blank like a 'possum's.

The mare lay beyond on the ground, her great eyes moist and sorrowful. Clabe had thrown down a basketful of shucks, but she had rolled away into soft dirt where the pigs had rooted. Father walked up to her. She trembled, though not moving in her agony. A spasm quivered her flanks. He put his hands on her neck for a moment, then the mare thrust a moist nose into his palms, and let her slobbering tongue hang between yellow teeth.

The mare began to strain, drawing her muscles into

cords, and I saw two small hoofs. Father stood over her, looping a grass rope around the colt's thin legs. I knew then the pain of flesh coming into life, and I turned and ran with this sight burning before my eyes, and my body cold and goose-pimpled. Standing behind the barn I was ashamed of my fear, though I could not go back until it was over. My humiliation was as loud as the guinea fowls crying in the young grass at the lot gate.

I did not go back until Father called me. Oates was watching and hadn't turned a hair. The children were on their knees looking between the fence rails.

The mare was standing now, mouthing the loose shucks. The foal rested in a pile of wheat straw. His spindling legs were drawn under him and the straws were stuck to his damp body. A horse-fly sang around his nose, and he swung his head, having already learned their sting. He looked at us gently and unafraid, then closed his eyes and laid his head on the ground. I hungered to brush the dark nose, to get near enough to touch the smooth flanks.

"If'n I had me this colt, I'd do a-plenty for it," I thought. "When his teeth growed out, I'd pull a mess of pennyrile and feed him every day till there wouldn't be a bone showing. I'd take a heap better care of him than Clabe Brannon, or Oates, or them dirty-faced children. I'd do a puore sight."

Oates approached the colt, but the mare drove him away, blowing through her nose, and lifting her heavy lips until yellow teeth were bared. The colt lay still, his eyelids closed.

"Colts hain't no good without proper raising," Clabe said, beginning to bargain with Father. "When he's weaned, I'd be right glad if you'd take and raise him. He ought to make a fine stud-horse."

"He's looking a little puny to me," Father said. "Ought to be standing up by now."

"I'd like the finest kind to give you something for helping out," Clabe said. "I shorely would, but they's not a cent on the place. I'm doing slim crapping this spring. Jist a couple acres. We et a passel of the seeds before planting time."

"I hain't charging my neighbors nothing," Father said. "I'm not a regular horse doctor, and got no right to charge. Anyhow, I don't reckon I've got a grain o' use for the colt."

Words were great upon my tongue, but with Clabe and Oates there, I could not speak them. My hope seemed a bloated grain of corn on a diseased ear, large and expectant, yet having no soundness beneath.

"I'd be right glad if you'd take him," Clabe said, knowing Father was stalling.

Father looked at Clabe. "If you're so powerful shore you want to get rid of him, I'll drap around some fine pretty day and fotch him home. Some far day when he's weaned and hain't bridle-scared."

Clabe and Father went into the barn. Oates spoke to me, showing his tushes. There was anger in his face, sitting dark as a thunderhead in his eyes. I knew he was angry about the colt, not wanting to give him up. "Pa's got a dram hid in the loft, I reckon," he said. He walked toward the lot gate, turning to look back at me, and I followed, going out by the pen where two razor-backs waded to their flanks in slop mud. We went into an old apple orchard, walking side by side. There were mushrooms growing pale and meaty under the trees. Oates kicked them as he walked, shattering the woody flesh of their cups.

"I heered tell mushrooms is good eating," I said, stepping carefully among them. "I'd like to try a mess cooked in grease."

"They ain't nothing but devil's snuff-boxes," Oates said, drawing his lips down sourly. "They're poison as rattlesnake spit."

A wren was nesting somewhere in the orchard. We

heard her fussing in the thick leaves, and we heard a cat sharpening her claws on the bark of a tree.

"Looky yonder at that there nanny cat setting in the crotch o' that tree," Oates said, his tushes breaking from his lips. "Paw wouldn't take a war pension for her, but she ain't worth a tick. She wouldn't catch a rat if'n they was a cheese ball hung around its neck. Once I took holt of her tail and wrung it right good. Now she has to climb a tree to sit down. You've seed nothing like that, I bet."

"I heered tell of a boy who's got a store-bought leg," I said. "He whittles on it for meanness, and once he driv a sprig in with a hammer, and a woman had a spell and fainted."

"That ain't nothing," Oates said, his lips turned accusingly. "I seed a man with one eye natural, and the other hanging down on one side of his face in a meat sack like a turkey gobbler's snout. Every time he winked that sack would jump a grain."

"I couldn't stood to look at it," I said. "It would be a pity-sake to have an eyeball growed like that."

Oates stopped under a tree, his eyes hard and his voice nettled. "I heered tell you Baldridges is spotted round the liver," he said. "Aus Coggins killed yore grandpap Middleton, and none o' yore kin done a thing to him. He's living free as wind."

"It's a lie-tale you heered," I said.

"It's gospel truth," he said. "I seed you run away when the colt was a-borning. And I brung you down here to show nobody's going to take him, now nor no time coming."

I stood looking at him, my eyes watering with anger, and for the moment I saw nothing except his tushes sticking out of his mouth, white and hateful, and his hands doubled into a rusty knot. Then he struck me in the face, and I struck back, wildly though with all my strength. We fought, swapping blows silently. Oates's nose began to bleed. He stepped back, his face twisted in fury. He searched the ground around us, picking up a stick of applewood fallen from a tree.

"I'll kill you graveyard dead," he said.

I did not move, and the stick fell swiftly upon my head, shattering in my ears like thunder. My knees doubled under me. Oates spoke, but I could not rise, and his words came as out of a fog, having no meaning at the moment though the words were clear and separate. Later, I knew what he said, looking back and remembering.

"Hain't no yellow-dog coward Baldridge going to get my colt," he said. "That there one's belonging to me, and I'd break his neck before I'd let him be tuck off."

After a little time I arose, feeling the knot on my head. Oates was gone. The wren was worrying among the leaves, chittering and fussing, knowing the cat sat in a tree crotch motionless as a charm. I walked toward the barn, not caring now whether I crushed the mushrooms underfoot.

Father stood with Clabe in the lot, looking at the colt. It was stretched upon the ground, its legs dry and stiff. The mare whinnied, rubbing her nose over the colt's body. I saw its eyes were open and staring. There was no life in them. The colt was dead.

"He must o' got hurt a-borning," Clabe said.

"A regular horse doc might o' pulled him through," Father said.

Father was ready to go. He looked at my swollen face, though he said nothing, and we set off walking down the creek, keeping to the left bank, where the cows had broken a path in the shape of their bodies.

I walked along bitter with loss, comforted only by the cruel wisdom that the colt had been spared Oates's rusty hands. Being seven on that day, and bruised and sore from fighting, the years rested like an enormous burden on my swollen eyes. We went on, not stopping or speaking until we saw our hill standing apart from all the others.

UNCLE JOLLY spent a night with us. He came riding Old Poppet late one afternoon, and she became so winded climbing the last steep of our hill he got out of the saddle, walking behind and pushing her rump.

"Yonder comes a fool," Father said, chuckling.

We ran through the stickweeds to meet him. Two guineas were strung across the saddle, legs tied and heads hanging down, squalling at every step. Uncle Jolly came into the yard, lifted the fowls off, stooped and came out between the mare's hind legs.

"He hain't no blood kin to me," Father said, and laughter came out of him like words spoken in a churn.

Uncle Jolly hung the guineas around Mother's neck, and hugged her, grunting big. "Thar's a couple buzzards Ma sent along," he said. "Says she tuck a notion to get rid of these last two. Can't sleep nights for all their potter-racking." And then he drew back, winking at Father. "Hell's bangers, Brack," he said. "You got nothing but a cornstalk of a woman here. I wouldn't have one lessen she was a good-sized armful." He shook Fletch, and pinched me, and stood looking at Euly. "The pretty girls nigh break their necks to kiss me," he said, "but plain ones allus sort o' hang back." He thumped her under the chin. Her teeth cracked together, and she looked scared.

"How's Ma getting along?" Mother asked. "I've been dolesome, hearing no word."

"Keen as a brier," Uncle Jolly said, "grumbling all the time, able to kick up a racket. Sometimes she has a stitch o' rheumatiz. I figure she'll be here to bury us all."

"Wonder she hain't gone crazy, the way you carry on, rag-tagging with the Law."

"I've been in jail just ten days this solid year. Feller drawed a knife on me and I gave him his front teeth to swallow, and a draft o' blood to wash them down with."

"What sort of crap you got in?" Father asked. "Quare time to be traipsing over the country."

Uncle Jolly eyed the weed-eaten slopes about our house. "A grain better'n you got, Bracky," he drawled. "My ten jail days came right at planting time. Too wet before, and too dry after. But I got me two acres in late corn. Out of dirt now, size of squirrel's ears. Ought to shuck enough this fall to make several gallons, and a couple pones of bread."

"Now, looky here . . ."

"I sot out on Ol' Poppet because Ma sent me. 'Son,' she says, 'you make a circle round and see how the chaps are. See Alpha, and Toll, and Luce. Tell them their ol' mommy is longing to set eyes on them agin. Tell them if'n they get out of something to eat, they's allus a dusting o' meal in my barrel.' "

"The mines hain't opened yet," Father said. "They're laying a new spur o' track, so it won't be long. No use stirring the top of the ground if you're going to dig your bread underside."

"I wouldn't work in a coal mine if there was gold tracks running in. I'll be buried a-plenty when I'm dead. Don't want bug-dust in my face till then."

Father jerked his thumb over his shoulder, pointing. "I got a right pretty garden, if I do say it."

Mother put the guineas under a washtub. One was a hen and the other a cock. "The pair ought to raise," she said. They kept sticking knobby heads flatways out of the crack left to give them air, sounding their metal voices. I shelled beans and pushed them under with a chip. Fletch tickled their feet with a straw.

While Father chopped wood to cook supper, Uncle Jolly came around the house-corner and beckoned to us. "Boys," he called, "I've fotched you wads of sap

gum from Lean Neck." He pulled two waxy balls
from his pocket. They were brown as buckeyes. "It's
good to chew," he said. "Better'n store-bought sweet
gum. Just you wet them with spit before champing
down."

I took one, and Fletch the other. They were soft as
dough in our fingers. Uncle Jolly's eyes got wide and
bright. He cocked his head, watching. We licked the
balls. We bit hard into them. Our teeth stuck, and
would hardly come apart. The gum spread. Uncle
Jolly laughed, his shoulders heaving, breath coming
out of him in gusts. He fell against the house, shaking.

Fletch began to cry. His mouth was gummed tight.
Uncle Jolly blew a great breath and stopped laughing. He thrust a finger far into Fletch's mouth, scraping the gum off his teeth. "That there's no way to act
when a feller pulls a rusty on you," he said. "Take hit
like a man, and start figuring on one to get even."

I raked my teeth with a stick, and we went to the
woodpile to see the martins dart around their pole.
They swarmed about the gourds in the evening air.
Uncle Jolly set Fletch on his knee, trying to make up
for the gum. He began to talk birds. Fletch's lips were
still puckered.

"Take me, now," Uncle Jolly said. "I like a wild living bird a sight more than a tame one keeping house in a gourd. Wild ones got a bushel more sense. They kin cut rusties same as a man. It's onbelieving what some kin do. I caught a wheedle-dee throwing his voice once, him setting in one tree, making out he was in another'n, and me looking my eyeballs out trying to see him.

"Now a towhee's got sense. I seed one last Tuesday setting on a limb, calling to his woman. 'Sweet-bird, sing,' he said, and his mate answered: 'I'll try, I'll try.' It sounded foolish like folks' talk.

"A towhee hain't a talking bird though. Split a crow's tongue, and it can larn to speak. But there's one bird talking is natural to. Over at Hardburly Mine a woman had a parrot-bird, fotched from West Virginia, or somewhere far yonder. Lived in a wire basket and had green feathers. I tell you its bill looked like a prong on a frog gig. They larnt it to speak words, and I hear it got where it could out-cuss her man. Hain't that a sight?"

Before dark Father took Uncle Jolly to the garden patch, wanting to show him the abundance there. They picked a dozen squashes for Aunt Sue Ella and Uncle Toll. Fletch and I hid behind the woodpile, trying to think of a rusty to pull on Uncle Jolly. We squatted in oak bark, scratching our heads, but we couldn't figure a one. I called Euly and she knew right off what to do.

"Set a couple of pin points in his saddle-seat," she said. "Push 'em through from the bottom."

"He'll think he's riding bobwire," I said.

"I bet too," Fletch said.

The saddle hung on the south wall of the smoke-house. Euly got the pins, but at that moment Father and Uncle Jolly came from the garden. Uncle Jolly had an early squash balanced on his head. He looked owlish at us. Fletch clapped his hands, and Euly and I grinned a speck. The squash fell to the ground. We didn't laugh. Uncle Jolly looked at us, wondering. Then he caught Fletch's arm, swung him to his shoulder, and carried him into the house.

"I'm scared Fletch will tell," Euly said.

"Now, no," I said. "He won't neither."

"Uncle Jolly might worm it out."

We stood a moment in the thickening dark. The martins crowded into the gourds.

"I'll fix it double," Euly said. "In the morning, early."

After supper Mother lighted the rio lamp, snuffing the smaller one we had eaten by. "Burns not a drop more oil," she said. The flame ate slowly around the cold wick. It coughed, and a thread of smoke went through the chimney. It sucked the oil upward, out of the clear bowl. The flame grew, it spread daywhite, opening its wings like a moth. The shadows leapt back, under the beds, behind the meat box.

Uncle Jolly blinked in the light. He leaned against a bedpost. "I stayed last night at Luce's place on Pigeon Roost," he said. "His woman's got the fanciest notions I ever seed or heered tell of. A chist o' drawers never sets in the same corner one week to the next. Little do-dacks here and there. 'Pon my word and honor, you can't stretch your arms withouten knocking flower pots over."

"Rilla's got four girls," Mother said. "They're a help, and don't mess like boys."

"When I walked in that house, she come a-sweeping a broom behind. I spit into the fireplace just to see her eyes crack."

"How's Luce making out?" Father asked.

"His woman's got him under the screw of her thumb. He knows to keep the money dribbling in, a day's work here, and one yonder. Log snaking, and stave planing. And not one furrow struck on his land. Got a horse-mule idle, eating his head off."

"You need a doughbeater to put the clamps on you," Father said.

"Aye, gonnies, I do now," Uncle Jolly said, yawning. "I'm ripe as a peach to get married. If'n a pretty girl blowed her breath on me, I'd fall off and squish. And they's one I'd be right willing to have shake my tree—Tina Sawyers, ol' Bowlegs Jabe's daughter, on Left Troublesome. But all his girls have got a way o' marrying Honeycutts. 'Pears to me they're cradle-claimed by Honeycutts."

"Now I wouldn't want to be family kin to ol' Bowlegs," Father said.

"Soon's I git my oats threshed, I'm going to start calling him Pappy."

Mother lowered the lamp wick. The flame sputtered, quarreling inside the chimney.

"I vow Luce's woman would give her right arm, square to the elbow, for a lamp like you've got here," Uncle Jolly said.

Mother lifted Fletch off the meat box where he had fallen asleep. She unbuttoned his breeches, putting him to bed in his shirttail. Euly got under the covers and shucked her clothes off, reaching them onto a chair. I crawled in beside Fletch. Uncle Jolly unlaced his boots, and Mother went outside. Euly buried her face in a pillow.

Father threw his brogans into a corner. He stepped out of his breeches, hanging them on a peg; he took off his shirt and rolled the long cuffs of his drawers down. "Which way did you go from the homeplace over to Luce's?" he asked Uncle Jolly. He spoke low, low as the frying flame on the wick.

"Shortest way across," Uncle Jolly said, "a-jumping from one rock to another like a goat travels. Had to nigh carry that Poppet over a couple of ridge butts. The saddle was on the wrong feller."

"I mean did you come along down Sand Lick by Aus Coggins' place?"

"I did. I hain't dodging nor surrounding nobody."

"Anything quare about his barn?"

"Burnt down. Fresh ashes, I noticed."

Father set his eyes on Uncle Jolly. "I heered it burnt, and I been trying to line who done it," he said. "That barn wasn't lightning-struck. Feller who lit the fire opened the stall doors and lot gates. The stock was driv out first."

"Don't look auger holes through me," Uncle Jolly said. "You hain't Judge Mauldin setting in court. I bet Aus won't be going before the grand jury saying I fired his barn."

"Aus's already enough scared of you Middletons. I reckon he's died nine times over thinking one o' you might plug him some day for killing your pap."

"Looky here, Brackstone. I hain't going to kill nobody less it's haft-to. That shooting was done when I was a chap, years ago. I bare remember. Now I'll scrap and tear up the patch, but I won't kill."

"Quare about that barn, I say."

Uncle Jolly snapped his galluses, looking scornfully at Father. "Good God, Brack," he blurted, "you don't wear them red wools the year round?"

"A summer cold is the worst kind," Father said.

"Better you keep out o' bull pens," Uncle Jolly warned. He jumped into the cot-bed by the wall. He lay there quietly for a spell, and when Mother came to blow the light, spoke up through the covers. "This here is the lonesomest tick I ever hit. No shucks talking foolishness in my ears." And later, whispering into the dark: "Brack, I gave them chaps wads o' cedar gum to chew, and they spit like adders."

"Twelve early squashes here for Toll and Sue Ella," Mother said, holding the jute poke in her hand. "Wisht I had something to send Ma."

"Ma said tell you she's got no catching disease," Uncle Jolly said. "There's no law agin folks coming to see her."

The sun-ball was an hour high. Uncle Jolly had bridled Poppet. He swung the saddle over the bony ridge of her back and stooped to fasten the buckle. He rubbed a hand over the padding, thumped the leather, and grinned. "Brack," he said, "these chaps are bright as blue-grass lawyers. Never tuck it after you though."

Euly held the baby, looking over its head at the saddle-seat.

Uncle Jolly put a foot in the stirrup. He glanced around at Euly and me. He keened his eyes, and twisted his mouth. He sprang upward, though not into the seat, coming down instead astraddle the mare's hips. Old Poppet jumped and whinnied, starting off at a gallop. Uncle Jolly squirmed, raising himself off the mare's back.

Euly tried to whisper something to me, but her voice was as shrill as the guinea hen's. "I put a handful of snatchburs behind the saddle," she said. She almost dropped the baby.

"There goes a born fool," Father said.

"WHEN it 'gins to blow around the north points of a morning," Father said, "sign it's going to weather."

Early summer rains set in before noon, the waters falling thick upon the hills. The draws filled, emptying downward. The martins hid in their gourds, swinging in drenched air. Little Carr rose, swelling through the willows, swallowing the green rushes. Damp winds whipped around the house, smelling of earth and water.

Mother set pans where the roof leaked. We pushed the beds catty-corner, away from the drips. Father sat on the trunk, the knots of his knees drawn under his chin. Fletch and I crawled on the floor, turning our faces upward, letting drops of water fall into our mouths.

Euly came from behind the stove, leaving the corn cob poppets to ask a riddle Mother had whispered to her. Her eyes lit up.

> Twelve pears hanging high,
> Twelve fellers riding by;
> Now Each tuck a pear
> And left eleven hanging there.

Father's face widened, for he knew the answer, having told Mother this riddle himself. Fletch looked at me, but I did not know how eleven pears could be left hanging. My head felt hollow.

"Hit was a chap six years old sprung that there riddle on me," Father said. "Taulbee Lovern's boy. Sharp as a sprig, that little feller is. Knows his figures square to a thousand, and says his a-b-abbs, back'ards and for-'ards. Hain't been school-taught neither. Never darked a schoolhouse door."

"I wisht I had me a pear," I said, still trying to solve the riddle. I was suddenly hungry. I closed my eyes and I could see a tree loaded with pears. Pears and paw-paws were the fruits I liked best.

Father glanced at Mother, his gray eyes burning in the woolly light. "Taulbee Lovern's boy it was," he said. Mother watched the baby sleeping at the bed-foot, never lifting her face toward Father.

"Who now is Taulbee Lovern?" Euly asked.

Euly's question hung in the room like the great drops of water growing under the shingles, stretching before dropping.

"Who is Taulbee Lovern?"

"Chaps too knowing are liable to die before they're grown," Mother said.

"As bonnie a chap as ever I saw," Father said. "Don't

reckon he's drawed a sick breath. Fed and clothed proper since he was born." Father's face got dolesome, and his voice lowered into the sound of rain beating the puncheon walls. He looked into all the corners of the room, at the two beds standing in the floor middle, at the empty meat box, at the ball of clothes piled on the table to keep them dry. He looked at Euly standing by the bedboard; he looked at Fletch and me squatting on the floor listening, our heads cocked to one side. "Three hundred acres o' land Taulbee has," Father said, "and a passel of that is bottom-flat. Six-room house with two glass windows in every dabbed room. Taulbee's tuck care of his own. They've never gone a-lacking."

Mother's face reddened. "I hain't complaining of the way I'm tuck care of," she said. "We hain't starved dead or gone naked yet. I'm not complaining. Now hush."

"Twelve pears hanging high," Euly began, but we were not listening.

"Who is Taulbee Lovern?"

The baby opened his eyes.

"Hush," Mother said.

Euly went back to her poppets behind the stove, speaking doll-talk to the cobs. I crawled between the meat box and the wall, going there to wonder about

Taulbee Lovern's boy, and how it would be to know square to the end of everything. I found a sassafras root, and I chewed it, spitting red juice through a crack in the floor. I wished I had a pear, one as mushy ripe as a frosted pawpaw. I felt I could eat the whole dozen hanging on the riddle-tree.

I licked flakes of salt off the meat box with my tongue. An ant marched up and down, feeling along the boards, and I saw four grand-daddy spiders. Three were tight in a corner, their pill bodies hung in a web of legs. A fourth walked alone. I took up a shoe and slapped the proud walker, and he went down, crushed upon the floor. He lay quivering in a puzzle of legs and body. As I watched, he rose up, moving into a cranny. I crawled away from the meat box, not wanting to see again the gray spot where he had bled.

Father held the baby in the flat of his two hands. Little Green stared into his face. "Take me," Father was saying. "I never tuck natural to growing things, planting seeds and sticking plows in the ground like Taulbee Lovern. A furrow I run allus did crook like a blacksnake's track. A sight of farming I've done, but it allus rubbed the grain. But give me a pick, and I'll dig as much coal as the next 'un. I figure them mines won't stay closed forever."

Euly brought a poppet for the baby to hold. He

looked at it gravely for a moment, clutching the cob in tallow-white hands, and then began to cry softly, a tearless, smothered cry.

"So puny he's been," Mother said, "I'm uneasy. He needs cow's milk, and plenty."

In the middle afternoon the rain slacked. We went out upon the washed earth, stepping on grass clumps to keep clear of mud. The swollen tide of the creek flowed high above the rushes, whipping the willow tops. A wet wind blew down into clouds banked against the hills. The martins came out of their gourds.

"Who is Taulbee Lovern?" Euly whispered into Father's ear. We heard.

"He was your mother's first beau," Father said, suddenly impatient. "Now hush."

Fletch ran to the woodpile, pointing at the gourds on the pole. "Look at that ol' martin-bird picking his teeth with a straw."

THE guinea hen nested in the pennyrile by the creek.

"Now where can that fowl be nesting?" Mother would say, and we would watch the hen run through the stickweeds, pecking left and right, taking flight at the least thing.

"She ought to have her wing-feathers clipped," Mother said.

"Nip the tip-wing joint," Father advised. "That'll keep her on the ground for life."

"A feather clipping is a-plenty."

We caught her at last, Fletch bringing her down from a high roost in the black birch where she had flown when we frightened her. Mother clipped the feathers of the left wing. She squalled, sounding like a rusty hinge. Afar off in the weeds the cock potter-racked fearfully.

"I wonder where she can be a-nesting."

One morning I saw a knob head lift in the pennyrile, and we knew. We went into the creek bottom, wading the tangle, searching.

"This would make the finest hayfeed ever was," Mother said. "Just going wasting."

Father kicked the lush growth where it caught the top hooks of his brogans. "I hain't started eating grass yet," he said. "There's not a beast on the place to be cutting it for, and it's the truth."

Mother set the baby down among the thick stems and he swung his arms about, squealing for joy. Fletch and Euly and I ran like young calves through the bottom, the pennyrile catching between our toes. We pulled armfuls, burying the baby in a green haystack. He laughed until tears rolled out of his eyes, and we stopped, not being sure why he cried.

"If we had us a cow her udders would be tick-tight," Mother said. "It would be a sight the milk and butter we'd get."

"Won't have use for a cow at Blackjack," Father said. "I hear the mines are going to open for shore. They're stocking the storehouse, and it must be they got orders down from the big lakes. This time of year they come, if they're coming a-tall."

Mother picked up the baby, holding him stiffly in the crook of her elbow.

"Where is them big lakes standing?" Euly asked.

"A long way north. It's onreckoning how far," Father said. "There's ships riding the waters, hauling coal to somewheres farther on."

"I had a notion of staying on here," Mother said, her voice small and tight. "I'm agin raising chaps in a coal camp. Allus getting lice and scratching the itch. I had a notion you'd walk of a day to the mine."

"A far walking piece, a good two mile. Better to get a house in the camp."

"Can't move a garden, and growing victuals."

"They'll grow without watching. We'll keep them picked and dug."

"I allus had a mind to live on a hill, not sunk in a holler where the fog and dust is damping and blacking. I was raised to like a lonesome place. Can't get used to a mess of womenfolks in and out, borrowing a dab and a pinch of this and that, never paying back. Men tromping sut on the floors, forever talking brash."

"Notions don't fill your belly nor kiver your back."

Mother was on the rag edge of crying. "Forever moving yon and back, setting down nowhere for good and all, searching for God knows what," she said. "Where air we expecting to draw up to?" Her eyes dampened. "Forever I've wanted to set us down in a lone spot, a place certain and enduring, with room to swing arm and elbow, a garden-piece for fresh victuals, and a cow to furnish milk for the baby. So many places we've lived—the far side one mine camp and next the slag pile of another. Hardburly. Lizzyblue. Tribbey. I'm longing to set me down shorely and raise my chaps proper."

Father's ears reddened. He spoke, a grain angrily. "It was never meant for a body to be full content on the face of this earth. Against my wont it is to be treading the camps, but it's bread I'm hunting, regular bread with a mite of grease on it. To make and provide, it's the only trade I know, and I work willing."

"I saw Walking John Gay once when I was a child," Mother said. "Walking John Gay traipsing and trafficking, looking the world over. Walked all the days of his life; seen more of creation than any living creature. A lifetime of going and he's got nowhere, found no peace."

"Woman nor chap nor beast he's got. None to provide for, no mouth to feed, living on bounty and beg. I choose mine work, the trade I know. I choose to follow the mines."

Mother's glance ran over the rich bottom, the hills rising bare out of it. Her words were hard and dry. "I say, see your satisfaction," she said, turning away.

Fletch had gone ahead, searching the pennyrile. Suddenly the guinea hen cried and flapped her wings, trying to rise from the ground. Fletch got on his knees, bending over the nest. We ran to it. There were twenty-six eggs.

"Don't touch a one," Mother warned, "or be blowing your breath amongst them. They'll be hatching soon. We can't move away to Blackjack till the young 'uns pip the shells. Leastways not till then. Hit would be a pity."

"It's me so thin that keeps the baby puny," Mother complained, "a-puking his milk, holding nothing on his stomach. If I got a scratch, I'd bleed dry. I need a tonic, fleshening me up, riching my blood."

Nezzie Crouch sat on the meat box watching Mother string tiny beans—beans too young to be picked. She had come from Blackjack to learn about our moving, walking three miles through mud to carry word back to the camp. The question waited in her eyes. She took a fresh dip of snuff, holding the tin box in her hand, and pushing the lid down tight. Three red tobacco leaves grew on the wrapper, sticking through the print.

"Well, now," Nezzie said, opening her stained mouth, "there's cures a-plenty for the picking. Ol' doc down at Blackjack says there's an herb for every ill, if you know what to pick and how to brew proper."

"Picking and brewing, I don't know which, nor how."

"I've heered tell a little 'sang is quickening to the blood."

"Woods full of 'sang there used to be, but I hain't seen a prong in ten year."

"So scarce it might' nigh swaps for gold."

"Don't reckon there's a sprig left on Carr Creek."

"Well, now, it ain't all gone. I seed a three-prong coming up from Blackjack, blooming yellow. I seed that 'sang standing so feisty, and I says to myself: 'Ain't that a sight? Nobody's grubbed him yet,' and I broke a bresh to hide it."

"Standing there belonging to nobody?"

"Nobody so far as I see."

"If I had that root, I'd try it."

"Belonging to nobody but ground and air. Hit growed from a seed the sky dropped. This chap can go piece-way home with me and fotch it back."

Nezzie worked a sourwood toothbrush in her mouth, pushing snuff into the pocket of her cheek. "I hear tell you're moving to Blackjack agin," she said. She had named it, looking over my head through the door, putting no weight on the words.

Mother finished stringing beans and hung the bucket on a peg, bringing out new-dug potatoes to scrape with the dull side of a knife. The potatoes were knotty and small. "The mines hain't opened yet, and we'll stay here anyhow till they do," she said.

"Tipple's been patched, and they're ready to start. Better chance of work if you're living in the camp."

"Brack might walk to and from the mine of a

day," Mother said. "Forever moving, I can't abide."

"There's a tale going round that you folks are nigh starved up here. I see you've got a fair garden patch. Not a grain of faith I put in such talk."

Mother's hands worked busily over a potato, the skin lifting paper-thin, wasting none of the flesh. "We've got plenty," she said. "A God's plenty." Her voice was as sharp as the bright blade of the knife.

The baby caught hold of the bedfoot and pulled himself forward, spreading his legs for balance. Nezzie watched, laughing to see him bend his knees. "Look how he tromps his foot, and hops up and down like a bird in a bush," she said. She bent over him, touching his pale face. "Hits little hide is so tender. You ought to make that 'sang tea for a fact."

THE guinea eggs hatched. The speckled fowls were as wild as partridges; they were as swift as granny hatchets. We rarely saw them. The grass tops shook where they fed. The metal clink of their voices grew. Once when it rained they roosted noisily under the house. We looked at them through a crack. There were fourteen biddies, and we remembered there had been twenty-six eggs.

"That ol' guinea hen hain't got a grain of sense," Mother said. "She's running them little 'uns to death, a-taking off through the weeds like a ruffed grouse, a-potter-racking and giving them biddies nary a minute to peck their craws full."

"That's their born nature," Father said. "Guineas are hard raising. Bounden to lose some. It's the same way with folks. Hain't everybody lives to rattle their bones. Hain't everybody breathes till their veins get blue as dogtick stalks."

"Next guinea eggs I set are going to be under a chicken-hen."

I chose a guinea, claiming it for my own, but afterwards I was never sure which was mine. Euly chose the smallest. Its feathers were covered with pale freckles; it had a ringed neck.

"Aye, now," Fletch said, sticking out his lips. "They are all belongen to me. I found the nest."

"Just so's I get in on the eating," Father said. "I bet one would be good battered and fried, tender as snail horns."

"They're not nigh big enough," Mother said. "Would be wasting meat."

Father lifted his head from the crack. There was hunger in his eyes, a longing for meat our garden patch could not cure. "If I had some bullets, I'd go hunt a coon," he said. "I saw tracks this morning."

"I've got a fine mess of squash cooking for dinner," Mother said.

Father sat on the meat box. "Recollect the time we had boiled gourds for dinner?" he asked.

"I do right well," Mother said, smiling.

"Tell, then."

"I come across four gourds one day growing behind the barn when we lived on Quicksand Creek. Yellow and pretty they were, looking a sight like summer squash, not having any necks to speak of. I cooked them on top of a big pot of beans."

"Oh, them beans tasted like a gall pie. Recollect?"

"Chickens wouldn't even touch them."

"A fowl's got a taster like folks. You never saw one peck a gourd."

Father pushed the meat box lid aside. He plowed his hands through the salt lumps. "Hain't even a pig knuckle here," he said. "This box holds nothing but a hungry smell." He dug deeper, straining the loose grains between his fingers. Something clung to his hand, a thin white stripping, a finger wide. "Looks like a johnny-humpback," he said.

It did look like a worm.

"Hell's bangers!" Father exclaimed. "It's a scrap o' meat." He rubbed the salt away and held it up. "Sow-belly," he said, and it was.

"Wouldn't fill your holler tooth," Mother said. "It's that little."

Mother washed the meat string. She held it over the pot. It dangled in her hand. We watched. It looked pine-blank like a johnny-humpback.

"Wait," Father said. "It's not big enough to give a taste to that pile of squash-mush. Bile it into a drop of soup for the baby."

"Fотсн the rio lamp," Father said. "I can't see by this blinky lantern."

Saul Hignight's calf had a cob in its throat and he had brought it to our place in the bed of a wagon. He lifted it in his arms, letting it down onto a poke spread upon the ground. It was a heifer, three weeks old, with teat buds barely showing.

I went after the lamp, but Mother feared to let me hold it. She put Green in the empty wood box and gave him a spool to play with. She lit the lamp and took it outside, standing over the heifer so that the light fell squarely where Father wanted it.

The heifer breathed heavily. Her mouth gathered a fleece of slobber. She looked at us out of stricken eyes.

"I'd brought her before dark," Saul Hignight said, "but I never knowed myself till after milking. I kept hearing something gagging and gaping under the crib. Figured it was a shoat at first."

"Hain't much milk to be got out of a cob," Father said. He pushed his right sleeve above the elbow and hitched it there. Saul wrenched the calf's mouth open and Father stuck his hand inside, up to the wrist. He wiggled his arm, reaching thumb and forefinger into the calf's gullet.

"Aye, gonnies," Saul said. "I fished for that cob till my finger nails wore down." His face flushed in the light.

We crowded around, looking over Father's shoulder. Slobber bubbled on Father's arm. He caught the calf's throat with the left hand and tried to work the cob into the grasp of his right.

"Slick as owl grease," Father said. "An eel hain't slicker."

The calf bellowed, a thin stifled bellow through her nose. Her legs threshed, her split hoofs spreading. She breathed in agony. Her fearful eyes walled and set.

Saul Hignight glanced suddenly at me. "Here, boy," he called, "help hold this critter." I moved slowly, fumbling. "Help hold!" Fletch sprang forward and caught the calf's hind legs, not flinching a mite. Saul glanced back sourly. I turned aside, though not being able to draw my eyes away.

Father pulled his hand from the calf's throat. "I can't reach the cob, for a fact," he said. "My fist is three times too big. Three times. Might be a chap's hand——"

"Here, boy." Saul twisted his head toward me. "Stick yore hand down to that cob, and snatch it."

I shook my head. Saul grunted and spat upon the ground. "The critter'll die while you're diddling," he said, his voice edged with anger. "Try it. I can't afford to lose this one."

"Me, now," Fletch said. He squatted on his knees. He worked his hand into the calf's mouth, and into its throat, nearly to the elbow. He grasped the cob and pulled with all his might. It wouldn't budge. The calf fell back upon the poke, gaping for breath. Her belly quaked.

Saul Hignight stood up. "Hain't a grain of use trying any more," he said. "She's bound and be damned to die. Born wrong cast o' the moon, I reckon." He clapped the dirt from his hands. "She'd a-made a fine little cow. Her mother's a three-galloner. She's proud stock."

There seemed nothing more to do. Saul whistled to his mules and they turned the wagon around, ready to start. "I can load the critter and drop her somewhere down the creek," he said. "She's good as dead and buzzard et."

"Let her be," Father said. "I might slick that cob out yet."

Saul got into his wagon. He clucked, jerking the lines. The mules set off into the dark. "You kin have the hide," he called back, "and the tallow to boot."

"If'n she dies," Fletch said, "they's pennies in the clock to put on her eyelids."

"If we could raise her," Mother said, "there would be milk for the baby." The lamp trembled in her hand; the tall chimney rattled the brass clasps.

"There's one way certain to get the cob," Father said. He weighed the chance in his mind. "One way shore as weather, but the calf might bleed to death." Mother and Father glanced at each other. Their eyes burned. "Bleed or choke," Father said suddenly, "what's the differ?"

"Let me try first," Mother asked. She handed the lamp to Father, warning him to hold it steady, not tilting the chimney. She put a hand into the calf's mouth, pushing the tongue aside, forcing the locked jaws apart, working feverishly. But she couldn't dislodge the cob. She had Euly try. Then she nodded to me. I knelt before the calf, looking into the cavern of its mouth, dreading to reach forth my hand.

"Hit's no use," Father said. "Fotch the hone rock, a needle, and a waxed thread."

Mother ran for them, knowing just where the hone lay between the logs, and where the needle and thread were. She came back in a moment, took the lamp and handed the hone to Father. She sent Euly into the house to stay with the baby. "He's fretted with being alone,"

Mother said. "Find him a pretty to play with."

Euly returned almost as quickly as Mother had. "I made Green a string crow's foot," she explained, "and tore a page from the wish-book for him to rattle."

Father drew a barlow from his pocket, snapping it open. He spat upon the hone and began to sharpen the blade with a circular motion, swiftly and with precision. The calf was weakening, being hardly able now to suck breath enough for life. Her eyes were lifeless and hard; she picked at the air listlessly with her feet.

The calf was turned to its right side, and the head lifted back. Mother reached the lamp to me, telling me how to hold it—close, and yet away from knocking elbows. "Both hands under the bowl," she said. She caught the calf's head between her hands. Father dug fingers into the calf's throat, feeling the proper spot, seeking a place free of large veins. The blade flashed in the lamplight; it slid under the hide, making a three-inch mark. Mother looked away when the blood gushed. It splattered on her hands, reddening them to the wrists. Euly began to cry, softly, and then angrily, begging Father to stop. "Begone," Father said. "You make a feller narvous."

The blade worked deeper, deeper. The horror of it ran through my limbs. It shook me as a wind shakes a tree. The lamp teetered, jiggling the chimney. Tears ran from my eyes, dripping from my chin. I couldn't wipe them away for holding the lampbowl. Father opened a space between the muscles of the calf's neck, steering clear of bone and heavy vein. The calf made no sound; only its hind legs jerked a bit. Fletch held to them, watching all that was being done, and not turning a hair.

At last Father put the knife aside. He eased thumb and forefinger into the opening, and jerked. The cob came out, red and drenched. It spun into the dark. The calf fell back weakly, though beginning to breathe again.

"Needle and thread!" Father demanded quickly. Mother reached it to him. Father folded the inner flesh and sewed it together, and then stitched the outer cut. And having done all, he looked at Fletch and grinned. "Here's a feller would make a good doctor," he said.

I handed the lamp to Mother so I could wipe away the shameful tears.

COLLINGSWORTH MINE loaded its first gon of coal the third week in June. Word came up the river, drifting into the creek hollows. Mothercoal Mine put fifty men to hauling fallen jackrock and setting new timbers. We heard that Father's cousins, Tibb and Harl, were there. The Hamlin blew its steam whistle one morning at three o'clock. The blast shook Boone's Fork, crossed He Creek and She Creek, lifting into the hills of the upper Kentucky River country. A shift of men was going into the mines for the first time in eight months. Roosters waked, crowing. Our guineas flew noisily out of the black birch.

Father got up and lighted a fire in the stove. The shagged splinters trembled in his hands. He piled in wood until flames roared through the rusty pipe. The top of the stove reddened, the cracks and seams of the cast iron becoming alive, traced like rivers on a map's face. Hoofs clattered along Little Carr before daylight. Men came down out of the ridges in ones and twos, hats slanted, riding toward Hamlin and Mothercoal. A pony went by, shoeless, feet whispering on rocky ground. A man rode barebones.

"They're wanting coal on the big lakes," Father

said. "It'll be going over the waters to some foreign country land."

After breakfast Father got his mine lamp, polishing the brass with spit and a woolen sleeve. "A long dry spell it's been," he said, "but they'll be working at Blackjack soon. Any day now, by grabbies. New tipple's been built. A fresh spur o' track laid to the drift-mouth. Patched the camp houses a sight too."

"It's only two miles to Blackjack," Mother said. "I figure you could walk it of a day. Pity to fotch the baby into the camps, and it so puny."

"We'll get a house yon side the slag pile this time, away from the smoke."

"Smoke blowing and blacking no matter where you set down in Blackjack Holler. I recollect the last time we moved to the camps. Tobacco cuds stuck in cracks, snuff dips staining the room corners, and a stink all over. I biled water by the pot and tub, washing and scrubbing, making it so you could draw a healthy breath."

"These chaps ought to be in school. Ought to be larning to read and cipher. No school closer to this place than Ol' Hargett Churchhouse on Lower Flat Creek. Three miles walking, if it's a foot."

"Larn more meanness than good in Blackjack school. Chaps a-cussing, fighting, and drawing knives."

"They run two teachers off from Ol' Hargett School last year. They've got a little smidgen of a man keeping there now. I figure he won't last the term."

"A moving is worse than a burning. Never'n I get me set down in a place and have a garden patch growing, than it's up and go."

"Living here, it'll be getting me home after dark."

"No place to graze the heifer in the camps."

Father started toward Blackjack. We watched him move along the creek road, his long restless stride eating dirt, pushing the distance back. The forkturn swallowed him, and we went into the garden to pick bugs. The baby crawled between the bean stalks, pulling at the runners. I gave him a wax bean to nibble with his new milk teeth. He gobbled it down, wanting more. I gave him a yellow tomato. He bit it, making a wry face. He sucked the tender pulp, and then cried because I would give him no more. Mother came from the far potato rows. She sat on a crab grass clump and opened her bosom. The baby jumped in her lap, beating tiny fists in the air.

"He's mighty nigh starved," I said, scared now about the bean and tomato.

Mother spoke, half aloud. "When your pap sets to work, I can buy a tonic. The baby will fatten then.

I've been drinking 'sang tea, but it does no good. Oh, I'm longing for the heifer to start giving milk."

I got more worried about the baby. I made a hickory sprout whistle for him; I tied a June bug's legs, letting him hold the thread while the bug flew around and around, wings humming like a dulcimer string. But he didn't get sick. He ate two bean leaves before I could snatch them away.

Father came home in early afternoon. His arms were full of brown pokes. We ran to meet him, even Mother going down the path a way. We grabbed the pokes he carried, running ahead, shouting up to Mother, holding the bags aloft. We emptied them on the table. There was a five-pound bucket of lard with a shoat drawn on the bucket. Brown sugar in a glass jar. A square of sowbelly, thin-rinded and hairy. A white-dusty sack of flour, and on it a picture-piece of a woman holding an armful of wheat straws. And there was a tin box of black pepper, and a double handful of coffee beans.

We looked in wonder, not being able to speak, knowing only that a great hunger stirred inside of us, and that our tongues were moistening our lips. The smell of meat and parched coffee hung in the room.

"I start digging tomorrow," Father said, drawing

himself tall and straight. The string of red peppers hanging from the rafters tipped his head. "They put my name on the books, and I drawed these victuals out of the storehouse on credit."

A lean hand reached toward the table, blue-veined and bony. It was Mother's, touching the sugar jar, the red-haired meat, the flour sack. Suddenly she threw an apron over her head, turning away from us. She hardly made a sound, no more than a tick-beetle.

Euly held the sugar jar over the baby's head, and he reached toward it with both hands. "Twelve pears hanging high," she said.

"We hain't moving down to the camp after all." Father was speaking. "Blackjack school won't be opening till fall sets in."

Father lighted a fire in the stove. I fetched three buckets of water from the spring, not feeling the weary pull of the hill, not resting between buckets. The knobby heads of the guineas stuck above the weeds, potter-racking. The smell of frying meat grew upon the air, growing until it was larger than the house, or the body of any hunger.

ON a July Sunday we went down Little Carr, turning up the ridge at the three linns, climbing the
cowpath through the ivy. The heifer bawled dole-
somely after us. We were going to Red Fox Creek.
Mell Holder had brought word Saturday night of a
letter in the post office there. " 'Brack Baldridge' hit
says on the kiver. Wore thin in mail pockets, searching for you," Mell said.

"Where now does that office set?" Father had asked.
"L T Pennington keeps a-jumping it around on Red
Fox."

Father carried the baby, Mother and Euly and
Fletch following after, walking single along the nar-
row path. I hung behind. I diddled, slow-footed, taking
my time. I peered into the brush on both sides of the
way. Under the ivy the ferns were still wet. They
waved like long green feathers; they breathed and
trembled, smelling of leafrot. Something there had nib-
bled the mosses, something small-muzzled and shy,
leaving no tracks. Higher, on the ivy tops where the
sun burned, bees worked the sticky blossoms. I heard
a wheedle-dee sing in the green dark. A sheaf of bark
creaked on a chestnut tree.

Mother's voice dripped through the leaves. "We hain't got a letter in three years."

"Aye-oo, aye-oo!" Fletch had cupped hands over his mouth, calling down to me. I climbed to where they waited under a shagbark hickory.

"Yearlings drive better in front," Father said. "You chaps walk ahead." The baby slept in his arms.

Beyond, at the mouth of Defeated Creek, we came on folk walking toward Seldom Churchhouse. The men wore white shirts, with collars buttoned. One had a latch-pin at his throat, for the button was gone, and another fellow's neck was wrapped around with a tie, rooster-comb red. The women walked stiffly, dresses rustling like wind among corn blades, their hair balled on their necks. They carried yard flowers and wild blooms in their arms: honeysuckle and Easter flowers, and seasash.

"Look," Euly said. "The men are carrying blossoms too."

A few held flowers tight in their hands, grasping them awkwardly. One carried a stalk cut from a meat-hanger center, white with flower bells. A fellow held a bunch of red clover blossoms, circling the stems with thumb and forefinger.

"Must be Graveyard Decoration Day," Father said.

"It's the second Sunday in July," Mother said. "I

reckon it's a funeralizing. They'll be preaching for sure. I'd give a pretty to hear a sermon. I would now."

We left the wagon ruts, coming onto the broad road. White pebbles, water-rounded and smooth, stuck between my toes. A horse went by, setting its feet down so quietly the rider hardly jiggled in the saddle. The church bell rang.

"We'll cool a spell in the churchhouse grove," Father said. "I'll take a look around to see if L T Pennington has come down from Red Fox."

Mother took the baby, and we sat down on a log.

A wagon drove among the poplars. The dry axles groaned, for one wheel was larger than the others, tilting the floor-bed. Three people sat on the spring seat, and six on chairs behind. The women held to the men's sleeves. The men had their hands latched to the siding. They drew up to the graveyard fence.

Father came back to tell us Preacher Sim Mobberly from Troublesome Creek was going to preach. "Folks here all the way from Rockhouse to Pigeon Roost," he said. "Got so many blossoms in that church, hit's like a funeral meeting."

"When I was a girl Brother Sim preached every burying of my kin," Mother said. "He's a saint if ever one walked God's creation."

"I never found L T Pennington," Father said. "I'll

just go along to Red Fox for that letter, and you all can stay for the preaching. No use dragging these chaps up thar and back."

"I've not got on a dress fitten," Mother said.

"I'm ashamed to go in barefoot," Euly complained.

Father grunted. He spat on the ground. "I don't reckon the Lord will be eying your clothes and feet. I'll be back against two hours." He went out of the grove to the pebbly road, striking upcreek.

We found an empty bench in a far corner of the churchhouse. Mother did not take us where the black-bonneted women gathered beside the pulpit. Men moved restlessly beside us; they sat before and behind, crossing and uncrossing their legs. Two whispered behind the flat of their hands. They were swapping knives, one taking boot in a cut plug of tobacco. The plug looked good enough to eat. It curled as though it had been sat upon in a hip pocket. The smell of it was heavier than the resin scent of the benches or the grave-yard flowers.

An elder stood in the pulpit. He was lean as a martin pole, thinner even than Father. His cheek bones were large, angled from the nub of his chin. He lined a hymn, speaking the words before they were sung, holding the great stick of his arm in the air:

Come, Holy Spirit, heavenly Dove,
With all thy quickening powers,
Kindle a flame of sacred love
In these cold hearts of ours.

The words caught into the throats of the hearers, and were thrown out again, buried in the melody. The hollow under the ceiling shook. A wind of voices roared into the grove. The second verse was lined, the third. . . . The elder raised on his toes, growing upward, thinner, leaner.

Dear Lord, and shall we ever live
At this poor dying rate?
Our love so faint, so cold to Thee,
And Thine to us so great.

"O God, have mercy." A moan came from where the black bonnets were. I rose on the bench, looking. I could see only the beak end of white noses bobbing out of dark hoods, the fans waving before them. "O God . . . sinner . . . I am . . . Lord."

The singing ended. A fleece of beard rose behind the pulpit, blue-white, blown to one side as though it hung in a wind. A man stood alone, bowed, not yet ready to lift his eyes. He embraced the pulpit block. He pressed his palms gently upon the great Bible, touching the covers as though they were living flesh.

His eyes shot up, green as water under a mossy bank, leaping over the faces turned to him.

"Brother Sim Mobberly," Mother whispered.

The preacher raised a finger. He plunged it into the Bible, his eyes roving the benches. When the text was spread before him on the printed page he looked to see what the Lord had chosen. He began to read. I knew then where his mouth was in the beard growth. " 'The sea saw it and fled: Jordan was driven back. The mountains skipped like rams, and the little hills like lambs. Tremble, thou earth . . .' " He snapped the book to. He leaned over the pulpit. "I was borned in a ridge-pocket," he said. "I never seed the sun-ball withouten heisting my chin. My eyes were sot upon the hills from the beginning. Till I come on the Word in this good Book, I used to think a mountain was the standingest object in the sight o' God. Hit says here they go skipping and hopping like sheep, a-rising and a-falling. These hills are jist dirt waves, washing through eternity. My brethren, they hain't a valley so low but what hit'll rise agin. They hain't a hill standing so proud but hit'll sink to the low ground o' sorrow. Oh, my children, where air we going on this mighty river of earth, a-borning, begetting, and a-dying—the living and the dead riding the waters? Where air it sweeping us? . . ."

A barlow knife cut into the seat behind us, chipping, chipping. A boy whittled the soft pine. The baby slept again, and Fletch's head nodded. The preacher seemed to draw farther away, melting into his beard. Presently his words were strokes of sound falling without meaning on my ears. I leaned against Mother, closing my eyes, and suddenly Father was shaking me. He held the letter in his hands. We went out into the grove, walking toward home. A great voice walked with me, roaring in my head.

"Whoever writ that letter spread on the curlicues," Father said. "Every word's got a tail, front and back. Can't tell where one ends and another'n starts."

"Jolly's name's signed," Mother said, "but it's not his handwrite."

"County court clerk writ it, I bet. It's like his scratching on tax receipts."

L T Pennington had read the letter to Father and he had remembered it word for word.

"That fool Jolly is in jail agin," Father said. "Dinnymited Pate Horn's mill dam two months ago, and now he's standing a chance o' being sent to the pen in Frankfort."

"Then Ma's setting at home alone, likely to take a sick spell any day, and nobody to tend the crops."

"One of Luce's girls is staying till school opens on Pigeon Roost. He wants us to send a chap to live with her this winter."

"Toll and Sue Ella ought to move in with Ma. They'd live better than they do, hand to mouth."

"Toll wouldn't hit a lick at a blacksnake. I'd a-soon have a hound dog piddling around."

Mother set her fingers into the ball of hair on her neck. "Pate Horn oughten to be damming the creek where he's got no right, holding back the waters, letting nothing up nor down."

"I figure the state pen will shave Jolly's tail feathers a grain," Father said. "Anyhow, I bet Aus Coggins will be tickled to have him shet up. I heard the other day Aus's fence has been cut a dozen times over, and his cattle making neighbor trouble. By grabbies, I bet Aus is tickled."

"Folks allus laying blame on Jolly," Mother said.

Father began to crack his knuckles, pulling his fingers one by one. "Mell Holder told me a quare thing the other day," he said. "Told it got where Aus Coggins can't get a stand o' corn on his land. Plants come up, then twist and die like they'd been burnt."

"I don't believe Jolly can witch ground."

"Stands to reason Aus is using a poison fertiliz'. But hit's truth he's tuck more punishment than Job."

THE flat fruit of the locust fell, lying like curved blades in the grass. August ripened the sedge clumps. Father began to come home from the mines in middle afternoon, no longer trudging the creek road at the edge of dark, with a carbide lamp burning on his cap. He came now before the guineas settled to roost in the black birch. We watched the elder thicket at the hillturn and plunged down to meet him as he came in sight. The heifer ran after us. Euly was the swiftest, reaching him first and snatching the dinner bucket Father carried. She hid in the stickweeds to nibble at the crusts in the bucket, scattering crumbs for the field-larks seeding the grass stalks. Fletch waited halfway down the path and Father would swing him to his shoulder, packing him to the house like a poke of meal.

After Father washed the coal black from his face we would eat supper. We heaped our plates with corn field beans. Our spoons dug into the mound until the top crumbled. "Eat till you bust," Father would say, grinning. The thinness had gone from his face and his shoulders were thickening again. Sometimes we took our victuals into the yard and the guineas latened their roosting to snatch the crumbs.

One evening in middle August Father sat on the battling block after supper, whittling a spool-pretty for the baby. "I saw Jonce Weathers, the Flat Creek school-teacher today," he said. "He was going along single stepping, like his bones was about to break at the joints. I caught up with him and he let off a spiel about being tired square to death. He did look a sight tender, and I reckon if he'd been laying flatback, picking slate out of a vein like I had all day, he'd been to bury. I asked him how many scholars he had and he says eighty-six, he thinks, but they wiggle so he couldn't count 'em for shore. I said I had two chaps ought to be in school. He says send them along, now he did."

Mother sat on a tub bottom holding the baby, watching Father notch the spool. "It's a long walking piece," Mother said. "Four miles one way. But I allus wanted my young 'uns to larn to figure and read writing. I went two winters to school, and I've been, ever since, a good hand to larn by heart. I never put my schooling to practice though, and I've nigh forgot how."

"I larned as far as 'baker' in the blue-black speller," Father said, "but I'm rusty on reading handwrite and print." He threaded a waxed cord through the spool hole, twisting match stems in the end loops until they pulled tight against his hand. The baby's eyes widened. When the spool was put on the ground it rolled along like a tumble bug.

The baby laughed, holding his hands for it, and stuck it into his mouth. He bit the spool with his milk teeth.

"No use putting off another day," Father said. "I told Jonce Weathers to nail another seat for you chaps."

Euly picked up the baby and ran around the battling block with him, running with joy. Fletch squatted on a broad chip, knowing he was only five, and too young to go. He cried a little, soundlessly.

AT seven o'clock next morning Euly and I sat on the puncheon steps of Old Hargett Churchhouse. We had gone early, meeting only miners on the creek road with their mud-stiff breeches rattling, their cap lamps burning in broad daylight. "Them's the brightest scholars ever was," one of the men said, "a-going to books ere crack of day."

Euly spoke her scorn, though not loud enough to be heard. "Dirt dobbers," she said.

The churchhouse door was chained and padlocked. We waited, looking across the foot-packed ground to the graveyard hidden behind a stickweed patch. A bushtail squirrel crept down a scalybark to wonder at us with bright eyes. "I bet he's tame as a house cat," I said. "I bet he is." Two bats flew around the eaves, disappearing with dull squeaks, and then we heard the dinner buckets of the scholars cracking together up-creek and down.

The children came into the yard and set their buckets by the steps. The boys crouched on their knees to play fatty hole, the bright marbles spinning from rusty fists into the dirt pockets. Euly went into the graveyard with the girls. I watched the boys, standing a little way apart. The losers held their knuckles to be thumped, clenching them against the pain.

A boy named Leth came up to me and said: "Let's me and you play big ring," and he loaned me two marbles: one to put in the ring, and the other to shoot with. I held them in the cup of my hand, and they were fine to look at—green as a moss pool, with specks like water fleas in the glass. He drew a great circle with the toe of his brogan. We squatted on our heels. I clenched a marble between thumb and forefinger, feeling its perfect roundness, smoother than any acorn.

"Yonder comes the teacher," Leth said, "but there's a spell yet before books. Jonce Weathers has got to clean after the bats. The floor gets ruint every night."

"Where, now, do them bat-birds stay of a day?" I asked.

"Yon side the ceiling, hanging amongst the rafters," Leth said.

We played two games of big ring, then we stood at the churchhouse door watching Jonce sweep with a brushy broom.

"Ain't Jonce the littlest teacher you ever saw?" Leth asked. "He's got scholars nigh big as he is. Be a wonder if he don't get run off. Two teachers they got rid of last year, and they'd a-made two of Jonce."

"I bet he's sharp as a shoe sprig," I said. "Size don't count for sense."

"I saw his arm muscle once," Leth said. "It wasn't much larger than a goose bump."

When the bell rang we went inside. I kept close to Leth, finding a place beside him on the bench where the primer children sat. Leth's feet touched the floor, but I could only reach it with my toes. The older boys came in late, the warped floor creaking under their steps. Jonce glared angrily at them. Books were opened, thumbs licked to turn the pages, and bright pictures spun under their hands.

"I've got no book," I said to Leth.

He held his so both of us could see. "We're reading *Henny Penny*," he said. "Look at that old dommer hen planting three grains of wheat. Ain't that a peck of foolishness? Fellow who writ this book is a witty."

"I can't read writing," I said, "but I know my letters."

"What's the biggest river ever was?" Jonce stood before the older boys, holding a book square as a dough board.

"Biggest river I ever saw was the Kentucky, running off to the blue-grass, and somewhere beyond."

"It's a river in South America, far off south, many thousands of miles."

"There's a place called South Americkee, over in Bell County. Now hit's the truth."

"This river is the Amazon. It's one hundred and sixty-seven miles wide at the mouth."

"I looked that word up in the dictionary and it said Amazon was a fighting woman. River or woman, I don't know which."

Cricket throb, dry and ripe, came through the window, dull against Jonce's words leaping over the room. He leaned from the pulpit, swinging his arms. Scholars stretched to draw numbers on the blackboard. Three classes in arithmetic were going at one time, three threads of voices intent as crickets. My feet hung from the bench, heavy as lead plumbs. "My tongue is dried to a string," I told Leth.

"Hold up one finger and crack the others," he said. Jonce saw me at last and nodded, and I went into the yard, being no longer thirsty where the air was free of bat smell and wood rot. I sat on a mossy rock under the scalybark, and the bushtail squirrel came halfway down, head foremost, unafraid. A titmouse whistled overhead, lonesome and questioning.

As I sat on the rock a boy ran out of the churchhouse, jumping the five doorsteps. His books were caught under his arm as he hurried down the creek road, leaving hat and dinner bucket behind. The squirrel fled up the scalybark; the titmouse hushed. Jonce came into the yard to look down the road after the boy. I slipped back into the schoolroom before he returned, wondering at the quietness there.

"Jonce put Bee Mauldraugh back in the fifth reader," Leth said, his voice husky with anger. "He reared up and Jonce cracked him with a figger book. Reckon Bee ought to be put back a grade, but I don't like to see nobody strike my kin. Uncle Hodge'll give Jonce trouble sure. He thinks the sun riz in that Bee."

Euly and I ate out of a shoe box at noon. We laughed when it was opened, amazed at what was there. Fried guinea thighs and wings, covered with a brown-meal crust. Two yellow tomatoes. A corn pone, and a thumb-sized lump of salt.

"Mommy must o' killed the guinea before daylight," I said. "I never heard a peep."

"I hope it wasn't my little ring-tailed one," Euly said. We had turned our backs on the others before looking into the box, but now we were not ashamed of what we had to eat.

"I couldn't stand to know I've eaten my little ring-tail," Euly complained, and gave one of her pieces away.

The children spread their food on the grass. They ate biscuits fist-big, with lean-streaked meat. Leth had milk in a dinner bucket. He crumbled corn bread into it, eating from the bucket with a wooden spoon.

Before the bell rang the girls went into the graveyard. The boys huddled together under the creekbank willows, burying their feet in damp sand, talking.

"I reckon we don't need to run Jonce off," John Winns said. "Hodge Mauldraugh will be doing that right soon."

"That Jonce has the quarest walk I ever saw," Eli Phipps said. "I'd give a pretty to see what kind o' run he's got."

The clapper shook in the bell. Leth got up, his marbles rattling in his pockets. "I like Jonce for a teacher," he said, "but I don't want to see nobody whipping my folks."

I walked across the yard with Leth. The older boys waited until the others were in the house before stalking in, clumping brogans on the floor. Jonce sat quietly in the pulpit, looking into a book that was a full hand thick. Pages flicked from his thumb. I looked up at him and saw his eyes run back and forth like an ant on a leaf. He stood up at last, grinning down at us.

"I've been learning about bats," he said. "They're unhealthy critters, festered with chinch bugs and lice, scattering plagues of diseases. And I learnt a bat's not a bird. It's a mammal, kin to man."

Whispers flowed over the room, protesting. "I'm not kin to a bat," a voice spoke. Leth nudged me with his elbow, frowning.

"We've been living in a bat house long enough," Jonce said. "Tomorrow I'll bring a poke of sulphur, and we'll give them a dose of fire and brimstone." Leth's eyes rounded. The older boys arose from their seats, grudges buried under the promise. "Four or five of you fellows bring mine lamps. We're going to have a bat-fly in broad daylight."

He came down out of the pulpit with the first reader in his hand, waiting until the scurry of voices died before sitting in front of our bench. Leth held his book before us. Henny Penny stood on the page, cackling, her comb red as a beet.

Jonce looked at me, and I was suddenly frightened. "Little man," he asked, "can you read in the primer?"

My tongue balled in my mouth. "I can't read words," I said, "but I know my letters."

"Fried guinea's breast in my dinner bucket," Father said. "I could hardly believe my eyeballs. I loaded two cars of coal extra after I'd et."

We were sitting on the woodpile, between supper-time and dark. Martins flew up from the lower ridges, where clouds were banked yellow as fall maples. There was still light enough for Mother and Euly to study the third grade spelling book. They sat high on the poplar logs, out of the baby's reach, for he wanted to pull at the pages.

"This speller's not belongen to me," Euly had said. "See what it says on the kiver, 'Property of the State of Kentucky.' "

"You won't be eating fancy victuals in the week middle from now on," Mother said. "I'm going to learn myself to spell the words I've forgot, and a sight o' them I've never come across. A body ought to be able to spell things they lay hands to every day, and things going by. Take them martin-birds flying there. I've seen martins all my born days, but I can't say the letters to their name."

"Kin you spell 'swampstem'?" Father chuckled.

"How do that word go?" Fletch asked.

"Crooked s, rugged m, s, t, 'swampstem.' "

Fletch laughed, popping his hands.

"I'm uneasy Jonce Weathers is going to get spelled down before the year is up," Father said. "They run two teachers off from Flat Creek School last year." Euly had told Father about Bee Mauldraugh, proud in knowing I was out of the room when Jonce struck Bee, and that I saw none of it.

"A little devilment is natural amongst chaps," Father said. "I'm not blaming the scholars. It's their folks forever tearing up the patch, putting fool notions in their heads. I figure a man ought to rack his own jennies, and stop piddling in other fellers' business."

"I allus wanted my chaps to read and spell and figure," Mother said. "Allus put a lot of store by that. Another rusty cut and they'll close the school shore. As long as we keep living here, Flat Creek School is their only chance earthy."

Night came up the hill, settling into the ridge pockets. The martins melted into the dark. "Time to hit the shucks," Father said, rattling poplar bark under his feet, but he made no move to go inside. The baby clucked where he sat between Father's knees.

I squatted on the chopping block, thinking of Jonce's promise. "If I had me a mine lamp, I could help scare bats," I said. "Bats a-hanging by the bushels in the churchhouse loft, messing the floor at night. Jonce is going to smoke them out tomorrow."

"Jonce says a bat ain't a bird," Euly said.

Father grunted. "I allus liked a flock of bats nigh," he said. "Mosquitoes and gnats live hard when they're roosting close around. I judge it's bad luck to kill a bat." He got up to go, swinging the baby on an arm. Green was so sleepy his head slid down into Father's hand.

We were on the road early next morning, going along with Father to the forkturn. The sun-ball broke out of the timber as we passed the mouth of Dry Creek. I wore an old mine cap with a carbide lamp hung over the bill, the round of the head pinched and fastened with a latch-pin.

Miners came down the creek, walking toward Blackjack. They looked at my cap, and batted their eyes at each other. "Aye, gonnies, if I don't believe Jonce is teaching them chaps to mine coal," one said. "Three we've passed wearing the gear."

When we reached the churchhouse most of the scholars were there already. The older boys had mine lamps, and carried snuff boxes filled with carbide lumps in hip pockets. The lamps smelled like burnt wool. Leth had a flambeau made of a rag stuffed in a bottle of coal oil.

Leth loaned me two marbles again, and they were the same ones—green as a catbird's eggs. I held them in the frog of my hand, clicking them together, watching the flea flecks sparkle.

"Them's the prettiest marbles ever was," I said. We squatted down to play a round of fatty hole.

"If you beat me out," Leth said, "they're belongen to you."

We played three games, and I lost them all. "You

can have them anyhow," Leth said when Jonce rang
the bell. "Reckon I've got a peck besides."

I caught the marbles up, trying to feel suddenly that
they were mine. In the deep of my pocket they felt
strange and cool against my leg, small and precious.
"I'm going to fotch you a hatful of chinquapins," I
said. "By grabbies, I am."

The big boys went in first, putting their lamps on
the water shelf, taking their seats expectantly. Jonce
glanced at the door, but there were no stragglers. He
counted the scholars, jabbing a finger toward each one.
"Not an absent or tardy scholar," he said. "Everybody
present like it was the last day of school." He leaned
out of the pulpit, elbows anchored on Preacher Claud
Madden's Bible. The classes began, chalk scratched
across the board, walking with giant letters, swelling
into words. Numbers, finger-counted, mixed with
things spelled. "R-a-m, ram, a brute sheep. . . ."
"Eleven plus nine comes to . . . twenty, I reckon."
"E-w-e, eouw, the one that drops the lambs. I had me
a lamb once I thought a sight of. Saved its tracks in
clay and got them yet."

We glanced at our mine lamps, thinking of bats
hanging under the roof.

Jonce saw Hodge Mauldraugh first. He came into
the churchhouse with Bee, standing there darkening

the door, saying no word. We looked back, stretching from our seats. The grass crickets were suddenly loud above the hush. Jonce came down from the pulpit, walking toward the door with the floor boards squeaking under his odd shuffle. He stood in front of Mauldraugh, his hands slightly lifted, open. Mauldraugh spoke, and his words were filled with cold anger. They poured out of him like sluice water.

"I'm not agin you reaching my boy back a grade," he said. "What he larns, I want hit got proper. But I'm agin my boy being whipped. I do all the scourging for my house. Nobody's going to beat my chap and keep drawing breath."

"I'm running this place," Jonce said. "Drawing pay to school keep and whip as I see fitten. When a scholar goes against the rule, I'll not spare the rod."

Mauldraugh spoke as though he had not heard, pushing Bee a little way toward Jonce. "I'm bringing him back to school," he said, "but I'd better never hear of him being touched. I'd better never hear . . ." He went out of the door, and Bee took a seat beside John Winns, glancing about, hard-eyed and proud.

The classes were doubled so all would be over by noon, and the afternoon free for the bat-fly. I learned to read the first page in the primer. "Henny Penny found a grain of wheat. . . ." I sat on my legs, for they ached from hanging over the bench without reaching the floor.

"Little man," Jonce said, "I'm going to hammer together a box for you to rest your feet on."

We ate hurriedly at noon. I had a lunch bucket of my own now, and sat with the boys upon the beech roots laid bare by creek flood. There was a baked horse apple in my bucket, oozing sugar from the top, and cushaw blooms, fried in meal batter, tasting like fish. We scattered the crumbs to the minnows working the shallows; we lit up our lamps.

Jonce dragged a ladder from under the churchhouse floor, setting it against the wall inside, beneath the trapboard. Eli Phipps went up first to slide the board away. We climbed after, grasping the creaking ladder slats, holding our lamps aloft. The floor gave under a step, nails prying loose from rotten wood. "Walk the joists, boys," Jonce said. "Likely to fall square through the ceiling." Below, the girls laughed, and the boys who had no lamps shouted from the ladder's end. Bee Mauldraugh's voice rose above them all.

The bats hung under the hip of the roof, higher than any of us could reach, wings folded against limp bodies. We held our lamps toward them. The mouse-furred patch gave no living sign. Jonce wedged a dishpan he carried between the joists. He poured a ring of sulphur in the pan, whittled a shingle, and started a fire. A smudge of gray smoke rose toward the roof, musty with burnt sulphur. The bats stirred, trembling, waving like old leaves.

The smoke grew until our lamps yellowed through it, and we began to cough. One bat fell, spreading the web of its wings before striking the floor. Suddenly they all came down, weaving drunkenly through the smoke, blowing about our heads. They flew swiftly, escaping at last out of the boxed eaves and through the traphole in the floor. The smoke thickened until our eyes smarted, and we hurried down the ladder.

The bats were gone when we got down. We put out the lamps, and wiped watery eyes with our sleeves. The scholars who had stayed behind were knotted around a bench, their backs turned to us, and there was none to see how proudly we came down the ladder. The scholars leaned closer to the bench, the joy of the bat-fly gone out of their faces. Jonce threw the hot dishpan into the yard and walked toward them, wondering. They stood aside as he came. Euly sat on the bench, holding a hand to her neck, her face white as beech bark. I was frightened, and the lamp fell from my hand.

"Bee Mauldraugh put a bat on me," Euly said. "It bit my neck."

Jonce's eyes searched the room, lighting on Bee standing against the blackboard, edging toward the door. Jonce sprang toward him, catching his sleeve as he crossed the threshold, and pushed him toward the pulpit. He caught up a willow pointer and struck Bee sharply across the legs, once, twice, and then Bee cried out in pain and anger, jerked loose, and leaped through a window. Jonce stood awkwardly with Bee's torn sleeve in his hand.

"Jonce ought never done that," Leth said to me. "He ought never touched Bee."

"Jonce ain't scared," I said. "Nary a grain, now."

"Uncle Hodge'll be coming," Leth said. "He vowed a feller ain't going to draw breath who whips Bee."

Jonce folded a handkerchief and wrapped it around Euly's neck. "Everybody can go home now," he said. "Everybody can go."

I went to the water shelf for my bucket, standing on my toes to reach the handle. As I pulled it down I heard a mousy noise. I stood on a bench and looked, and there was a bat in the shelf corner. I opened my bucket and popped it in, closing the lid tight. I walked out of the churchhouse with Euly, Leth coming behind us.

"It's not more than a quarter mile up to Uncle Hodge's place," Leth said. "He'll be coming soon."

The scholars stood at the graveyard fence, looking up the creek road where Bee had gone. Euly, crying a little, caught hold of my hand. "I ought never told," she said. "It's ruint our only chance earthy."

Hodge Mauldraugh came down the cove road, walking slowly, walking with his right hand in his hip pocket, wrist-deep and bulging.

"Uncle Hodge ain't going agin his swear word," Leth said, and his speech was anxious, justifying his kin.

I looked at Leth and I saw then that he had Mauldraugh eyes, like Bee's. I stood apart from him, hating him suddenly. I drew out the two marbles he had given me, dropping them at his feet. They lay on the ground, green as millet juice, but he did not pick them up or look where they had fallen.

Hodge came into the churchhouse yard, bending a little to search the windows. We heard his feet clump on the front steps, the floor boards rub under his weight, and a pistol shot. I turned and ran down the creek road, sick with loss, running until there was no wind in my body. Euly came swiftly behind, soundlessly as a fox runs.

We climbed the hill to our house in early afternoon,

standing breathlessly at the door, looking in at Mother playing with the baby. I pulled the lid off my dinner bucket and the bat soared out, swinging like a leaf in the wind.

"B-a-t, bat," Mother said.

II

FALL had been dry and the giant milkweed pods broke early in September. Lean Neck Creek dried to a thread, and all the springs under the moss were damp pockets without a sound of water. Father had sent me over from Little Carr to stay with Grandma while Uncle Jolly laid out a spell in the county jail. Though Grandma was seventy-eight, she had patched two acres of corn. Even with the crows, the crab grass, and the dwarf stalks she had made enough bread to feed us through the winter. But there would be little for the mare. The hay-loft was empty and the corn-crib a nest of shucks.

Uncle Luce sent word from Pigeon Roost that he would come to help gather the crop. Grandma's bones ached with rheumatism and she was not able to go again to the fields. She sat in the cool of the dogtrot, dreading the sun. We waited through the parching days, pricking our ears to every nag's heel against a stone in the valley, to the creak of harness and dry-wheel groan of wagons in the creek bed. Field mice fattened in the patches. Heavy orange cups of the trumpet vine bloomed on the cornstalks, and field larks blew dustily from row to row, feeding well where the mice had scattered their greedy harvesting. We waited impatiently for Uncle Luce, knowing that when he came we should hear from Uncle Jolly, and that Uncle Luce would take the mare home for the winter.

"It's Rilla that's keeping him away," Grandma said. "Luce's woman was always sot agin him doing for his ol' mommy. I reckon Luce fotched her off too young. She wasn't nigh sixteen when they married."

We waited for Uncle Luce until the moon was full in October. The leaves ripened, and the air was bloated with the smell of pawpaws where the black fruit lay rotting upon the ground. 'Possums came to feed there in the night, and two got into a box trap I set above the barn. We ate one, steeped in gravy, with sweet potatoes. I shut the other in a pen, Grandma saying we would eat it when Uncle Jolly got home. She was lonesome and spoke of him through the days. "I reckon he's a grain wild and hard-headed," Grandma said, "but he tuck care of his ol' mommy."

One morning Grandma said we could wait no longer for Uncle Luce. She took her grapevine walking stick and we went into the corn field. We worked two days pulling corn from the small hoe-tended stalks. When all the runty ears were gathered she measured them into pokes, pulling her bonnet down over her face to hide the rheumatic pain. There were sixteen bushels.

"We won't be needing the barn this time," she said. "We'll just sack the puny nubbins and put them in the shedroom."

With the corn in we waited a few days until Grandma's rheumatism had been doctored with herbs and bitter cherry-bark tea. Then there were the heavy-leaved cabbages, the cushaws and sweet potatoes to be gathered. The potatoes had grown large that year. They were fat and big as squashes. Grandma crawled along the rows on her knees, digging in the baked earth with her hands. It was good to see such fine potatoes. "When Jolly comes home he'll shore eat a bellyful," she said.

I ran along the rows with a willow basket, piling it full and spreading the potatoes in the sun to sweeten. Once I ran into a bull nettle, and it was like fire burning my bare legs. I scratched and whimpered. Grandma took a twist of tobacco out of her apron, chewed a piece for a few minutes, and rubbed the juice on the fiery flesh. "You hain't big as a tick," she said, "but you're a right smart help to your ol' granny."

The days shortened. The air grew frosty. Nights were loud with honking geese, and suddenly the leaves were down before gusts of wind. The days were noisy with blowing, and the house filled with the sound of crickets' thighs. There were no birds in the bare orchard, not even the small note of a chewink through the days.

Before frost fell we went to Grandma's flower bed in a corner of the garden and picked the dry seeds. We broke off the brown heads of old maids and the smooth buttons of Job's tears hanging on withered stalks.

"There's enough tears for a pretty string of beads," Grandma said, "and enough seed left for planting."

Later we pulled and bundled the fodder in the field, stripping the patches for the mare in her dark stall. "If Luce don't come, Poppet is going to starve before the winter goes out," Grandma said. "It's Rilla hating me that keeps him from coming. Oh, she'll larn all her children to grow up hating their ol' granny."

Uncle Luce came after the first frost. He came whistling up the path from Dry Neck with the icy stones crackling under his feet. Since the gathering, Grandma had been in bed with rheumatism in her back, getting up only to cook. Uncle Luce was full of excuses. Rilla was sick. It was getting near her time. His four daughters had had chicken pox. "I'm hoping and praying the next one will be a boy-child," Luce said. "A day's coming when I'll need help with my crap. Girls hain't fitten to grub stumps and hold a plow in the ground."

Grandma noticed Uncle Luce's hands were blackened with resin and asked if he'd been logging. "I had to scratch a little something to buy medicine for Rilla," he said. "My crap never done nothing this year. Planted late, and never got the proper seasoning. I reckon I'll be buying bread before spring."

"I was reckoning you'd take the mare home for the winter," Grandma said. "I was thinking you could ride her back to Pigeon Roost."

"I hain't got feed for my own beast," Luce said. "I'll be buying corn for my horse-mule before another month. Poppet has already et more than she's worth. She must be twelve years old. The day's a-coming you'll need another nag to crap with. It would be right proper to take ol' Poppet out and end her misery."

Grandma raised up in anger. "Luce Middleton, if you was in reach I'd pop your mouth," she said. Then she lay back and cried a little. Uncle Luce went over and shook her, saying he never meant a word about Poppet. He wouldn't shoot her for a war pension.

Uncle Luce didn't say a word about Uncle Jolly until Grandma asked him. She waited a long time, giving him a chance to tell her without asking. "You hain't said a word yet about your own brother," Grandma said. "It's about time you told." Then we learned that Uncle Jolly's trial had come up the last of September, and he had been sentenced to the state penitentiary for two years. "I'll get Toll to move in with you next March," Uncle Luce said. "I figure he'd be right glad to come. He's renting land anyway. And his wife would be a sight o' company."

"No," Grandma said. "I'll make out. This chap can stay through to spring, and maybe on into summer. My children I've worked and slaved for have thrown their ol' mommy away. Now that I can't fotch and carry for them, they never give me a grain o' thought. I've been patient and long-suffering. The Lord knows that."

Grandma began to cry again.

"I figure you'd fare better with Toll than Jolly," Luce said. "Toll is solid as a rock and never give you a minute's worry. Jolly is a puore devil. He jumps in and out of trouble like a cricket. Puts me in mind of a hound dog trying to lay down on a shuck. I hope the pen will make him pull his horns in a little."

Grandma's voice trembled as she spoke. "He hain't mean to the bone, and he's the only one of my boys that looks after me. I'm afeared I won't live till he gets back. I pray the Lord to keep me breathing till he comes."

Grandma was quiet when Uncle Luce got ready to go. She brought out a string of Job's tears she had been threading. "It might pleasure Rilla to have them," she said. "It might help with her time coming."

During the short winter days the sun was feeble and pale, shining without heat. Frost lay thick in the mornings, and crusts of hard earth rose in the night on little toadstools of ice. Footsteps upon the ground rang metal clear, and there was a pattern of furred feet where rabbits came down out of the barren fields into the yard. My 'possum rolled himself into a gray ball in his pen, refusing to eat the potatoes I brought him, and then one morning I found him dead. His rusty, hairless tail was frozen as stiff as a stickweed. The mare grew gaunt in her stall, and there was not a wisp of straw left underfoot. I gleaned the loft of every fodder blade, and the crib of shucks. I filled the manger with cobs, but she did not gnaw upon them, choosing instead to nibble the rotting poplar logs of the wall. I led her down to Lean Neck every day, breaking a hole in the ice near the bank. After a few days she would not drink, and I began to take a bucket of water to the barn. I fed her a little corn—as much as I dared—out of our nubbin pile in the shedroom.

The cold increased and the whole valley was drawn as tight as a drum. The breaking of a bough in the wood shattered the air, the sound dropping down the hills, striking against icy ridges. In the evenings I took an old quilt to the barn and covered Poppet. I dug frozen chunks of coal out of a pile beside the smokehouse for the fire, and when it seemed there was not going to be enough to last the winter through, I went up on the mountain beyond the beech grove and gathered small lumps where the coal bloomed darkly under the ledge. The fire was fed from my pickings until snow fell, covering all trace of the brittle veins.

There were days when Grandma was too sick to rise. I baked potatoes, fried thick slices of side meat, and cooked a corn pone in a skillet on the hearth. We used the coffee grounds until there was no strength in them. When the meal gave out I shelled corn and ran it through the coffee grinder. It came through coarse and lumpy, but it made good bread.

As Grandma grew better she would sit in bed with a pile of pillows at her back. She slept only at night. During the day she was busy listening and counting. She knew how many knots there were in the ceiling planks. She could look at a knot a long time and then tell you a man who had a face like it. Most of them were old folks, dead before my time, but there they were. There was one knot that looked like Uncle Jolly. Grandma used to look at it by the hour. "I'm afeared I'll have to piddle away my days looking at this knot-picture," she would say.

One day she counted the stitches in the piece-quilt on her bed. They ran to a count I had never heard. "I larnt to figure," Grandma said, "but I never larnt to read writing. My man could read before he died, and he done all the reading and I done the figuring. We allus worked our larning like a team of horses." We had no calendar, but Grandma counted the number of days until Uncle Jolly would get out of the penitentiary. "It's nigh on to six hundred and fifty-five," she said when the figure work was done. The time had not seemed so long before. Now it stretched along an end- less road of days.

There were hours of talk about Uncle Jolly. Grand- ma said he had held no old grudge against Pate Horn. Grandpa used to log with Pate. Uncle Toll had mar- ried one of Pate's daughters. It had been the dam he built across Troublesome Creek that Uncle Jolly hadn't liked. The fish couldn't jump it, and none could get into Lean Neck to spawn. He sent Pate word to open one end of the dam until the spawning season was over. Pate didn't move a peg. Uncle Jolly went down one day and set off two sticks of dynamite under the left bank, blowing out three logs. He went down, with daylight burning, to blow that dam up.

"Jolly ought not to done it," Grandma said. "Hit looks like the Lord is trying my patience in my last days when I'm weak and porely."

Near the middle of December the mare stopped eating the nubbins of corn I took her. She would mull her nose in the bucket of water without drinking and roll her moist eyes at me.

I opened her stall door and let her wander into the midday sunlight. She did not go far, lifting her leaden hoofs through the snow, turning from the wind. Presently she went back into the stall and stayed there with her head drooped and her eyes half closed. One morning I went out and found her stretched upon the shucks. Her nose was thinly sheeted with ice. She was dead. I latched the stall door and did not go back to the barn again that winter.

January was a bell in Lean Neck Valley. The ring of an ax was a mile wide, and all passage over the spewed-up earth was lifted on frosty air and sounded against fields of ice. Icicles as large as a man's body hung from limestone cliffs. Grandma listened to the weather noises when her work was done. She was better now. At times when the wind was not so keen she cooked on the stove instead of the fireplace, but it was hard to keep warm in the drafty kitchen.

One Sunday Grandma heard a nag's hoofs on the path to the house. It was Uncle Toll from Troublesome Creek. He brought a letter from Uncle Jolly and he read it to us. His face was dull with worry. Uncle Jolly was coming home. There had been a fire in the prison. "Mommy, do you reckon he broke jail during that fire?" he asked. "He hain't nigh started his term."

"Jolly is liable to do anything he sets his mind to," Grandma said. "He allus had his mind sot on looking after his ol' mommy. I reckon he'd do anything to get free." And now there was no joy in his coming. There was nothing to do but wait, and those three days before he came seemed longer than any count Grandma ever made.

Suddenly he was there one morning, hollering to us from the yard. There was Uncle Jolly. He had slipped up on us, and even Grandma had not heard him come. He stood before the door, his eyes bright as a thrush's. He had on a black suit, and a black hat with the pinched crown sitting at an angle on his head. We sat looking at him, awed, not moving. He jumped into the room and grabbed me in his arms, pitching me headlong toward the ceiling and bumping my head against the rafters. It hurt a little. He jerked Grandma out of her chair and swung her over the floor. She was laughing and crying together. "For God's sake, Jolly, don't crack your ol' mommy's ribs."

Then he was all over the house, prying and looking. He opened the meat box and sniffed into it. He thumped the pork shoulder we had been saving. "Ripe as a melon," he said. "It smells like Kingdom Come." He reached elbow-deep into his pocket and drew out a knife. It was a big one. With a single blade open, it was nearly a foot long. There was a blue racer with a forked tongue carved on one side. "I made that in the workshop," he said. "They never knowed I was making it." He swung it through the air, striking toward me. *Plunk* it went into the pork shoulder. Uncle Jolly was devilish like that. Grandma was already sifting meal, and he cut a half-dozen slices of meat to fry.

Uncle Jolly found the corn in the shedroom. He picked up one of the runty ears and pinched a grain. "Is this all you raised?" he asked.

"We got some mighty pretty cushaws," Grandma said. "The sweet taters done right well too."

"The mare will starve on this corn," Uncle Jolly said. "You know what I'm going to do? I'm going to buy ol' Poppet a sack of brought-on sweet feed, mixed with molasses and bran. I reckon her teeth is wore down to the gum."

He began to gather ears to take to the barn.

"Just you wait, son," Grandma called. "Just you wait till we get dinner over." Grandma looked hard at me. I didn't say a word.

When we sat down to the table, Uncle Jolly began to eat with both hands. "I hain't had a fitten meal since I left Lean Neck," he said. He loaded his plate with shucky beans and a slice of meat, talking as he ate. "I stayed at Luce's house last night," he said. "Luce and Rilla's got another girl-child, born three weeks ago."

Grandma laid her fork by and stirred in her chair. "Is Rilla getting along tolerable?" she asked.

"Rilla is up and doing. They named the baby after you, Mommy. They named it Cordia."

Grandma blinked, making a clicking noise with her teeth, speaking. "It's good to have grandchildren growing up honoring and respecting their ol' folks."

"Oh, Uncle Jolly," I begged, "tell us about the jail fire and how you got free."

Uncle Jolly swallowed, the raw lump of his Adam's apple jumping in his throat. "It was the biggest fire ever was," he said. "It caught the wood shop and tool sheds, and it was eating fast. It might o' got the jail-house if I hadn't stayed there and fit it with a water-spout. Everybody else run around like a chicken with its head wrung off. Then the Governor heard how I fit the fire and never run, and he gave me a pardon. He sent me word to go home."

Grandma settled in her chair. "It was dangerous, son," she said. "It might o' burned the jail. Whoever sot that fire ought to be whipped with oxhide. Some folks is everly destroying and putting nothing back. Who lit that fire, son?"

Uncle Jolly's mouth was too full to answer. He dropped his eyes and swallowed. "I sot it, Mommy," he said. He took another slice of meat and heaped more beans on his plate. Grandma sat quiet and watching, her blue-veined hands clasped in her lap. Her face was sad, but her eyes were bright with wonder.

"You know what I done coming up Troublesome Creek this morning?" Uncle Jolly asked suddenly. "I pulled another log out of Pate Horn's mill dam. There's a good-sized hole now. The perch will be swarming into Lean Neck this spring." And when he had finished eating, pushing his plate back: "I hear Brack Baldridge has moved into the camps, moved off that hillplace he owns down to Blackjack."

"EIGHTEEN SIXTY-EIGHT it was," Grandma said, and her words were small against the spring winds bellowing in the chimneytop. She spread her hands close to the oak-knot fire. They were blue-veined like a giant spider's web. "That was the year the pigeons come to Upper Flat Creek, mighty nigh taking the country."

I squatted on the limerock hearth before an ashhill where the bread pone baked, holding a broomstraw to know when it was done. Uncle Jolly had gone to Hardin Town to buy salt and victuals, and we had not eaten since morning. Hunger heaped inside me, higher than the ashhill where the bread was buried.

"Them pigeon-birds were worse than a plague writ in the Book," Grandma said. "Hit was my first married year, and Boone and me had grubbed out a homeseat on Upper Flat, hoe-planting four acres o' corn. We'd got a garden patch put in, and four bee gums working before I turned puny, setting in wait for our first-born. I'd take a peck measure outside and set me down on it where I could see the garden crap growing, and the bees fotching sweetening. There was a powerful bloom that year, as I remember, and a sight of seasoning in the ground."

Bread smells thickened in the fireplace, and I stuck the straw into the ashhill. It came out with a sticky lump on the end. My hunger could hardly wait the slow cooking. I turned my head so Grandma couldn't see me eat the dough from the straw.

"Hit was early of a May morning when the pigeons came," Grandma went on. "A roar sot up across the ridge, and Boone came down out of the field, looking north where the sound was. We waited, dreading the wind tying knots in the young corn, but nary a cloud we saw. The sound got bigger, and nearer. 'Hi, now, you git inside,' Boone said, and I did, fearing my child would bear a mark. I allus followed my man's word when I was puny. I looked through the wall-crack and saw the first pigeons come down the swag. Light brighted their wings; wings rock-moss gray, and green underside. Then they came in a passel. The sun-ball was clapped out, and it got nigh dusty dark. Boone, he took a kindling-wood stick, knocking at them that flew low, drapping four. After a spell they were gone, and we had breasts of pigeon for supper, fried in their own grease. They were that fat. Boone allus was a fool for wild meat. 'Hi, now,' he said, a-cracking bones betwixt his teeth, 'I'd give a pretty for a pot-pie cooked out o' these birds.'

"Kite Thomas come up Flat Creek before dark, saying he'd heard the pigeons had done a sight of damage to the craps over at the Forks. He had a poke of sulphur and was going to the doublings three miles yon side the ridge where the roost was. 'A sulphur smudge will bring 'em down,' he said. 'I'm a notion salting a barrelful. My woman feeds nothing but garden stuffs of a summer. I allus like a piece o' meat alongside.' Boone wanted to go, but knowing it was near my time, he never spoke of it. 'A pigeon pie would make good eating,' he said. 'I figure on eating me one before them birds traipse off.'

"Kite and Boone went outside, and I heard Kite laughing. He went off a-cackling like a guinea-hen. I got sort of dizzy, and tuck to bed. Pigeon-birds kept a-flying round in my head, thundering their wings. I tuck the big eye and never slept a wink that night."

Wind drummed the chimney. A gust caught the oak-knot smoke, blowing it into our eyes. A sift of ashes stirred on the hearth. I tried the bread again, the straw coming out slowly, though clean. I raked a bed of coals closer to the ashhill with the poker.

Grandma balled hands on her knees, waiting until the smoke thinned and the ashes settled. "Hit was the next day the birds came a-thrashing through the hills," she said. "I was setting in my garden, guarding it agin the crows, when I heard a mighty roaring, like a tide on Troublesome. Boone was in the corn patch, so I never went inside, wanting to get a square look at the birds. I never gave a thought to me being so puny. In a spell they come o'er the ridge, flying low down, a-settling. A passel sot down in my garden and began to eat and scratch. I run up and down hollering, throwing clods and crying. Hit was like trying to scare a hail-storm. The birds worked like ants, now. I run and hollered till I couldn't, then set me on the ground, feeling sick to die.

"Next thing I know I was in the house, and thar was a granny woman setting beside the bed, holding something wropped in a kiver. Now I knowed what was in that thar kiver, but I was scared to look. Boone came in laughing, and said it was a boy-child. Hit was Toll, our first-born. He brought the little tick to the bed, and I couldn't wait to look, asking: 'Has it got a mark?' 'No mark particular,' Boone told me. 'His left hand hain't natural though.' The kiver was opened and thar the chap was, hits little face red and wrinkled. Boone pulled the left hand out, and on the side was an extra finger-piece, no bigger than a pea, having nary a nail nor jint. I cried, looking at it.

" 'Hit won't be thar for long,' Boone vowed. He got his razor and 'gin to strop hard, putting a hair edge on the blade. When I knew what he was going to do, I let

in hollering and screaming worse than I did when the
birds tuck my garden. The granny woman held me in
bed, and Boone tuck the baby into the kitchen. I listened, catching for a sound of the baby. He never made
one. I reckon it never hurt much. Boone brought him
back and thar was a drap of water in its eyes.

"The granny woman cooked a pigeon pie for supper. But I couldn't touch a bite. I've never et a bird
since."

The bread was done. I raked it out on the hearth,
blowing ashes from the crust. When it was broken the
goodness of it filled my eyes and throat. "A pair o'
pigeon wings would go good with this bread," I said.

Grandma looked hard at the bread, then broke a
piece for me, taking none for herself. She took the
poker and shook the oak-knot fiercely. "I hain't a grain
hungry," she said.

"I BORE eight chaps, and not one died of a bullet," Grandma said. She sat on a three-legged stool beside the hair trunk, speaking of Grandpa Middleton and times past, speaking and looking the while for a piece of cloth to make a coat. My pea jacket had greened with wear, the elbows shredded beyond patching, worn to a sorry cloth broomstraws could be pitched through.

"Eight me and Boone brought into this world, and every one a wanted child. Four died young, and natural. Three boys and one girl we raised. My boys were a mite stubheaded, as growing ones air. But nary a son I had pleasured himself with shooting off guns, a-rim-recking at Hardin Town and in the camps, a-playing at cards and mixing in knife scrapes, traipsing thar and yon, weaving drunk. Nor they never drew blood for doing's sake, as I've got knowing of. Feisty though, and ready to fight fair fist if the other feller wanted it that a way. I allus said, times come when a feller's got to fight. Come that time let him strike hard where it'll do the most good, a-measuring stick with stone, best battler win. The devil can't be fit lessen you use fire."

Grandma stirred old garments with her hands. A

mellow smell came out of the trunk. It swept the room. She lifted a white cotton shirt, crackling with starch. The collar was stiff as a harness.

"Boone's. I saved it a-purpose for recollection. It punishes me to look, though there's comfort in the keeping, a punishing comfort."

Two bags of quilt pieces were lifted next; and then a pair of socks, gray and woolly, and old.

"Boone wore them on his dying day, on the day Aus Coggins tuck his life for no reason on God's square earth."

"Shot Grandpa plumb through?" I asked, hungry to hear more.

"Shot so his life's blood flowed a river. Yonder, up Lean Neck where the road comes off the hill and crosses the creek, years ago. The spot is marked, I hear. Marked peculiar. A locust post was driv on the spot, and I hear it tuck root. I've never been thar to see. Never."

"Fired his rifle-gun for no reason a-tall?"

"Boone sold Aus Coggins a nag and it died with bloats the night after. Et cribfeed till her belly smothered her heart. Aus went crazy mad, saying the nag was sick a'ready when bought, saying she'd been doctored to die. He was allus one to scatter blame. Aus bushwhacked the road, waylaying Boone as he came home from Whitesburg. Boone had been yon side Rockhouse Creek to sell my weave work. They had hard words, I reckon, and Aus up and shot. Up and shot out of his hurt pride, and for no reason earthy."

"Died sudden, or strung out?"

"His coming to death I never inquired. I never asked, child."

I remembered Oates Brannon's accusing. His words grew loud in my ears. "*Aus Coggins killed yore grand-pap . . . living free as wind . . . yellow-dog cow-ards . . . Middletons . . . Baldridges.*"

Grandma's eyes were damp. Her chin quivered as she ran hands swiftly amongst the packed-away things. Questions hung on my lips, but she turned from them, thrusting them back with a fury of searching, of seeming forgetfulness. The hair trunk was peopled with keepsakes and recollections. She held up things for me to see, naming, giving them meaning.

"An applewood button box your grandpa whittled. Kept all my babies' latch-pins in it. This puore silver thimble, it was fotched across the waters by my gran'. Fotched o'er from England in ol' times.

"A turkey caller Boone made, but now they hain't a wild one these hills over. A few pheasants, but nary a gobbler.

"You've never seed a pretty like this, child. A Tennessee pearl. Growed in a river mussel shell. A beau gave it to me, when I was twelve and marrying age. I was forever thinking to put it on a ring band to wear. The fairest pretty I've got."

Grandma lifted a coat, holding it by the shoulder-tips. It was red, and beautiful, and near my size. I could not believe such a fine garment would be wasted on my back. I spoke, looking meanwhile at the coat, thinking back. "Had they been a horse doctor to tend that nag, they'd been no dying, man or beast." I drank in the redness of the coat, wondering why it lay in the hair trunk. "They're doctors for folks when they're ailing, and they ought to be one for beasts." I looked away and there were red specks before my eyes from long looking at the bright cloth. The icy rime on the windowpane seemed to redden. I longed to stick my arms through the warm sleeves of the coat and go running into the cold: I would stand where the wind bittered the stiff fields, caring not a whit for all its blowing. "I'm a-mind to be a horse doctor when I grow to a man. I am, now. I been a-figgering."

Grandma reached into the elbow-deep pockets, emptying them of cedar shavings. "Moths live hard where you keep sweetwood," she said. Her hands flicked in and out. "This coat belonged to my second boy, Vester. I made hit to pleasure him in his last sickness. Brewed a pot o' madder roots to dye red, madder being far and beyond the warmest color. A wee shike-poke of a child Vester was, and thin, thin. But he bore the same countenance as his father, a sight noble to see. When he sunk low and was gone, I saved this one piece."

I tried to think of Vester, a slim knuckle-knob of a fellow, my size and age; but I remembered Oates Brannon instead: Oates and I walking under the apple trees, stepping small amongst the mushrooms, and the old cat with a broken tail worrying the birds. I remembered Oates's tushes, and heard his words again. "*You Bald-ridges is spotted round the liver . . .*"

I measured the coat with my eyes, feeling no hope of wearing it. A recollection of Vester, to be saved ever-more. And I kept hearing Oates speak his hateful words. I stood up suddenly, filled with a great anger. "A wonder Aus Coggins's still alive," I blurted. "A wonder Uncle Jolly——"

"Try the coat," Grandma commanded. I held my cuffs and slid arms through the sleeves. It was a full body fit, coming to my knees, though the sleeves were short, barely to wrists. I felt warm as a bag of wool. "Now stand where I can see the fitting," Grandma said. "I've got a thing to tell you."

I waited, as a mollygrub waits inside its fleeced hull.

"On Boone Middleton's burying day I had my boys promise. They tuck oath on the Book. Tuck it every one except Jolly, he being only twelve, and too young for swearing. I said: 'There's been blood shed a-plenty. Let Aus Coggins bide his time out on this earth. Fear will hant his nights. Hit'll be a thorn in his flesh. Let him live in fear. He'll never prosper nor do well. Let him live in sufferance.' I said this, and more."

Grandma began to cry. A mousy sound came through her nose. Water beads hung on her cheeks. "You're the spit image o' Vester in that coat," she said. "Hit'll pleasure me no end to see you wear it." She caught arms around me, putting her face against my sleeve. And when I drew back, ashamed to be hugged, she lifted her head and her eyes were damp and bright. "Child," she asked, "where'd you strike the quare notion to be a horse doctor?"

BEFORE a tip of green showed in any brushy place you could feel spring growing through the sky. The robins came early, cocking heads in the cold. The gray bodies of goldfinches yellowed, for all the world like pussy buds blooming. And where no other sign held on wood or field, finger twigs of elder and willow and service swelled beneath their hull of bark.

"If I was stone blind, I'd know a new season was coming," Grandma said. "This time o' year the rheumatiz strikes my hips. The pain sets deep and grinds. Five of my chaps were born in the spring and that might be the causing." She took to bed for a spell, and Uncle Jolly cooked for us morning and evening. Of a morning he would arise at three o'clock to make coffee and hoe-cakes before walking four miles to snake logs for Elias Horn. He had need of this work. Money for meal, meat, salt, and a tonic for Grandma had to be got. His hands blackened with resin that would not wash off no matter the amount of scrubbing, and Grandma complained bitterly, seeing his grubby fingers poking in the dough. It plagued her to lie abed, helpless. "When spring opens," Grandma said, "I'll be up and doing. Three days' sun, and I'll be well enough to beat this feather tick and hang it to sweeten."

One morning I saw a redbird sitting in a plum bush, its body as dark as a wound. "Spring's a-winding," I told Grandma. "Coming now for shore."

"Even come spring," Grandma said, "we've got a passel of chills to endure: dogwood winter, redbud, service, foxgrape, blackberry. . . . There must be seven winters, by count. A chilly snap for every time of bloom."

I wished for the thaw and greening, for I longed to go home. No word had come since Father moved to Blackjack. Few travelers turned down Lean Neck from the creekhead road, choosing the steep climb over the ridge rather than the far way around, and there was no one to ask. During those lonesome days I wondered about Blackjack, picking bare my memory of it. I remembered going there once with Father, remembered the houses crowded in the hollow with paths between, miners tramping toward the drift-mouth, caps lit and dinner buckets hooked to belts. It was like a place dreamt. There now was our house, a dark, boarded camp house; Fletch and Euly, and Mother, Father, and the baby living inside; our beds, the stove, the meat box sitting in strange corners. Did Euly and Fletch go to the Blackjack school? Had the baby learned to speak words? Had the heifer started giving milk?

"Do you reckon Green can walk by now?" I asked Grandma.

She looked at me gravely, seeing how homesick I was. "Why, child," she said, "he's bound to walk in time, bounden to rise up and find his own way. Gee-o, I'm punishing to try walking agin myself."

And then she talked a sight, more than was good for her, wanting to wear the dolesomeness out of my mind. "I'd give a pretty to see Alpha's last child. I would, now. Hain't seed him, nor Rilla's last 'un, nor Sue Ella's youngest. Never they come and bring their biddy ones. I'd give a pretty." She sat in bed, quilt-covered knees under her chin, looking back many a year. "I recollect your ma when she was a chap. A tidy body, good to mind and help. Housekeeping or field work, so quick she whisked a broom or hoe-chopped, never one could keep alongside. She could trash any of her brothers in a corn row. Fair she was, though a mite thin, to speak the truth; fair as a wild bloom. A choose and pick she could o' had amongst the fellers. First, Laird Todd, Clark Millen, and Joe Quinn tried to keep her company, but nary a thing she'd have to do with them. 'They hain't a man good enough for her,' I told her father.

"Luster Ross asked for her hand. Asked Boone if he'd agree to having him for a son-in-law. Luster Ross, who was heiring more land than a stick could be shuck at, coal lands big companies were trying to buy, asked her to be his bride. Aye nor nay Alpha answered, caring not a grain for all his leather boots and proud horses. A different beast he rode every visit; a fine coat he wore on his back, and his pockets rattled silver every step. He's rich now beyond counting. Owns mines, and opens and closes them as he fits. Threeseam Mine. Hardstay. Lizzyblue. Got part ownership o' Blackjack Mine. I hear he's got pastures full o' racing horses in blue-grass country. Gambling horses. Lives in a house size of a hilltop, and never dirts his hands.

" 'Your daughter is overweening in her pride,' Boone kept saying. 'Overweening like the Book says.' And now I wonder. A sight of fellers gave Alpha the eye, I tell you. Colter Hollowell rode time and agin all the way from Licking River in Rowan County; and Taulbee Lovern from Hardin Town, and Cleve Arnett from Big Leatherwood. Upstanding families, good stock. Now they's one feller your pap allus was jealous of. Taulbee Lovern. Oh, Boone'd quarrel at me the way Alpha acted toward him, but never a word to her. 'She must be waiting to marry the King of England,' he'd say."

"I've heard of Taulbee Lovern," I said. "He's got a boy that's the brightest feller ever was. Spells and reads writing, and never darked a schoolhouse door."

"Alpha could o' had rings on her fingers and combs in her hair," Grandma said, "but along come Brack Baldridge from Tribbey Camp, a long, lean, strung-out person. Him she tuck. Married a coal digger, a mole-feller, grubbing his bread underground. For gold and silks, she'd no fancy, and I was right glad for a fact. But allus I'd wanted her to choose one who lived on the land, growing his own victuals, raising sheep and cattle, beholden to nobody.

"Now, nary a word I'd say agin Brack. He's good to work. Hain't scared to bend his back nor mud his boots. Chap, you've got a clever pappy. Brack's an honest man, but heired sorry kinfolks. That Samp, and them two devil cousins diddling around, stirring trouble. Hit's no wonder Brack's forever moving, abiding nowhere long. Only if he'd settle some place and grow roots, I'd not be eternally worrying."

I put a beech log on the fire and poked the charred embers underneath. A covey of sparks winged into the chimney. I sat on my stool and homesickness was hot inside of me.

"Child," Grandma said, "hit would comfort me to know you'd never be a miner." She lay back on the pillows, resting a bit. The feather tick swallowed the weight of her body. "I'd give a year out o' my life to see all my children and their chaps," she said at last. "A year's breathing I'd give. Never they come to see their mommy. Old, and thrown away now. No good to fotch and carry for a soul." Anger rose in her throat. She struck her elbows against the tick. "When my dying day comes I'm right willing to be hauled straight to Flat Creek burying ground and put beside my man, buried down and kivered over against any o' my blood kin was told. My chaps won't come when I'm sick and pindly; they hain't use in coming to see me lay a corpse."

Her voice lowered, the anger creeping away. "Child," she said, "I long most to see Baby Green. I hear Alpha sets a store o' love for him that's ontelling. More than's good, for if he was tuck to die, it'd be more than could be borne." She closed her eyes, shutting away the damp sad glance of pain.

I RAN into the fields one April morning, thinking to climb to the bench land where Uncle Jolly was breaking new ground. The sky was as blue as a bottle. A rash of green covered the sheltered fence edges, though beech and leatherwood were browner and barer still for the sunlight washing their branches. I began to climb, hands on knees, the way being steep. I went up through a redbud thicket swollen with un-opened bloom and leaf, coming at last to where Uncle Jolly was plowing. The bench spread back to the swag, level as creek land, set up against air and sky and noth-ing. Uncle Jolly had already broken a half-acre of furrows in the rooty earth with the horse-mule Uncle Luce had loaned him.

"Whoa-yo," Uncle Jolly said when he saw me. He drew rein and leaned against the plow handles, blow-ing. He whistled a long redbird whistle. His forehead was moist, his shirt stuck to his back. He'd been hus-tling the mule, and was glad of the rest. "Hain't you got a sup o' water?" he asked.

"I never thought," I said. "I come up to learn to plow."

A drop of sweat hung on Uncle Jolly's chin.

"Jumping Josie!" he said. "This fence-rail beast

would pull you clear over the plow handles."

"Now, no," I said. "I'm a-mind to learn."

He grinned, scratching into the thick of his hair. "A chap never larnt too young," he said. "Just you fotch a jug of spring water, then I'll try you a furrow." He hung the reins about his neck and leveled the plow. He dug a shoe toe into the black dirt. "Aye, God, this land'll make," he said. "It's rich as sin."

I brought the jug of water. Uncle Jolly crooked a finger in its ear, swinging it upon his shoulder. He drank loud swallows. Water ran down his neck; it drained thread streams under his collar. He lowered the jug and stuck his tongue out. "Seems a bull frog's swum here," he said. "Hit's sort o' wild." He took another long drink. I reckon he drank a quart. "I allus liked a wild taste—the wilder the better," he said.

"What's this mule's name?" I asked.

Uncle Jolly sat the jug by. "Banged if I know," he vowed. "Luce told me, but I can't recollect. Ought to be named Simon Brawl, he's so feisty."

A flock of goldfinches circled the new ground, their gay song sowing the air. *Per-chic-o-ree, per-chic-o-ree, per-chic-o-ree.* They settled at the field's edge and it was as if the dry stickweeds had suddenly burst yellow blooms. They pecked at seed heads; they rattled empty pods of milkweed stalks.

Uncle Jolly glanced over the plowed land. The furrows were straight as a measure, running end to end without a bob. "Hain't many folks know how to tend dirt proper," he said. "A mighty spindling few. Land a-wasting and a-washing. Up and down Troublesome Creek, it's the same. Timber cut off and hills eating down. Hit's alike all over, Boone's Fork, Little Carr, Quicksand, Beaver Creek, Big Leatherwood. . . ."

"I want to learn proper," I said.

"What's folks going to live on when these hills wear down to a nub?" Uncle Jolly complained. He lifted the plow, setting the point into the ground. I stood there, not knowing what to do. "Best you walk betwixt the handles and get the lay," he said. I got between, holding the crosspiece. Uncle Jolly grasped the handle ends and clucked. The mule didn't move. He whistled and shouted, but the mule paid no mind. Uncle Jolly grinned. "This fool beast won't move lessen you call his name, and that I can't remember." He tried a string of them. "Git along, Jack! Pete! Leadfoot! John!" He reached down and caught up a handful of dirt, throwing it on the mule's back. The mule started, skin shivers quivering his flanks. "It's like that every time I stop," Uncle Jolly said. "A horse-mule stubs pine-blank like a man."

The earth parted; it fell back from the shovel plow;

it boiled over the share. I walked the fresh furrow and
balls of dirt welled between my toes. There was a smell
of old mosses, of bruised sassafras roots, of ground new-
turned. We broke out three furrows. Then Uncle
Jolly stood aside and let me hold the handles. The mule
looked back, but he kept going. The share rustled like
drifted leaves. It spoke up through the handles. I felt
the earth flowing, steady as time.

We turned the plow at the end of the third row.
"This land's so rooty," Uncle Jolly said, "I'm going to
let you work over what I've already broken. You can
try busting furrow middles. Strike center, giving left
nor right, and go straight as a die."

I grasped the reins and handles. "Get along," I called,
big as life. The mule didn't budge. He lifted his plugged
ears and looked back at me, sly and stubborn.

"He's a regular Simon Brawl all right, with steelyard
peas for hoofs," Uncle Jolly said.

The mule started after I threw dirt on him. He went
down the first row peart enough, ears standing end-up,
for Uncle Jolly began singing at the top of his voice.

> Oh, I had a little gray mule,
> His name was Simon Brawl,
> He could kick a chew terbacker
>   out o' yore mouth
> And never tetch yore jowl.

I plowed three furrows and pride swelled in me as sap blows a willow bud. It was like being master where till now I'd only stood in awe; it was finding strength I'd no knowing of. When I doubled back on the fourth row, I saw Uncle Jolly sitting on the ground, leaning against a chestnut stump amidst the stickweeds, his eyes closed to the sun. The mule saw Uncle Jolly too, and his ears drooped. He began to walk faster. The harness rattled on his bony body. The furrow crooked a bit and I got uneasy. "Hold back thar," I shouted, but he didn't mend his way.

At the fifth row's end I looked anxiously at Uncle Jolly, hoping he would take over. One glance and I saw he had gone to sleep. I was ashamed to call. The mule hastened the furrow, the plow jiggling, scooping dirt, running crooked as a blacksnake's track. I jerked the lines. I shouted all the mule names I'd ever heard. The share hooked a root and the reins pulled from my hands. The plow jumped a furrow, rising alive-like. And then I called Uncle Jolly, being at last more frightened than ashamed.

We no longer bore north and south. The mule cut northwest, southeast, back and forth, catty-cornered. My feet flew over the ground. We plowed a big S. We made a long T, crossing it on the way back. I reckon we made all the book letters. We struck into the unbroken tract, gouging a great furrow, around and around, curling inward, tight as a watch-spring. I couldn't shout or raise a sound. There was no wind left in me.

A voice sprang across the bench. "Hold thar, Bully!" The mule stopped in his tracks, and I went spinning over the plow. I got up, unhurt. A bellow came out of the stickweed patch; it was a laugh near too big for a throat to utter.

I looked in time to see Uncle Jolly rise to his feet, then crumple to the ground. He threshed among the weeds, his arms beating air, laughing in agony. He jerked; he whooped and hollered. He got up twice, falling back slack-jointed and weak. A squall of joy flowed out of him.

And when Uncle Jolly had his laugh out, he came across the field, weaving drunkenly. The mule watched him come, lowering his head, acting a grain nervous. Uncle Jolly sniggered when he reached us, and I saw a fresh throe boiling inside of him, ready to burst. The mule raised his head suddenly. He licked his yellow tongue square across Uncle Jolly's mouth.

"I bet that there's a wild enough taste," I said, scornfully.

"SHE's a traipsing fool," Uncle Jolly said, jerking his thumb toward Grandma. "I never saw the beat, a-setting out agin daylight, treading the dark, God knows where."

It was July. Grandma sat before the kitchen stove, drying the morning dew from her shoes. She sighed a little, being tired from her walk, and watched Uncle Jolly grit roasting ears for breakfast. He had brought a dozen down from the bench field and cornsilks were scattered about like brown locks of a woman's hair.

"It's no wonder rheumatiz's driving sprigs in your bones," Uncle Jolly complained. "There I was, coming off the bench, me thinking you were abed, and beholt! You come doddling along the ridge."

Grandma wove her hands together on her knees. "I been walking on these legs seventy-eight years," she said. "I'm figuring to walk a few more miles. I hain't going to set around and let rheumatiz tie 'em in a pinch knot. Hain't wear that breaks a door hinge, hit's rust."

"You put me in mind o' Walking John Gay," Uncle Jolly grunted. He rubbed a small-grained ear over the gritter. Corn milk drained into the pan, washing the shreds into the batter. He was going to fry fritters.

I asked: "Who is Walking John Gay? Somewhere I heered that name."

Uncle Jolly didn't answer, wanting Grandma and me to think he was angry. He threw a cob across the room into the wood box and grabbed another ear, ripping it over the gritter. The table was splattered with corn milk. Suddenly he jerked a hand away, whistling between his teeth. He jabbed a finger into his mouth.

"Just take your time, son," Grandma counseled. "Hain't nobody starving to death."

Uncle Jolly chose another ear, spinning it on the gritter. His nose wrinkled, but he didn't laugh. He puckered his lips; he looked as mean-mad as he could. "A little flesh and blood mixed in the batter ought to make fritters taste a sight better," he said. "They hain't more than a half-acre o' bark skinned off my hand."

"Where does Walking John Gay live?" I asked.

"Wherever he pegs his hat," Uncle Jolly grumbled. "One thing though, he's got sense to do his walking of a day. Ma goes hoot-owl hunting night-times. Oh, I've seed Walking John a dozen times over, meeting him places you'd never expect to see a body. Once I went a-courting on Redbird River, and I come on him walking along pitching pebble-rocks, keeping six in the air, catching and a-pitching. And I says: 'Looky here,

John Walkabout, where air ye forever going? What air ye expecting to see you've never saw yet? Hain't the head o' one holler pine-blank like the next 'un?' "

"Once he come walking along Lean Neck Creek," Grandma said. "I recollect it was Ruling Day in February, years ago. John Gay was mighty nigh froze teetotal. We punched the cannel-coal fire till it was white hot, and he sot there groaning while he thawed. Boone got him to eat a snack at the table. He wiggled in the chair, not being broke to taking ease, punishing to go.

" 'Now just hold your horses,' Boone told him. 'I got a bundle o' questions to ask you who've traveled these mountains.' And he 'gin to ask a sight: 'What about them bee-gum rocks in the breaks of the Big Sandy? Tell where's that beech tree standing Dan'l Boone whittled his name on? I'm blood kin to ol' Dan'l. Have you seed a single pair o' wild pigeons the earth over?'

"Boone asked questions till dark. I fed the stock and milked. I done all, and when I went in they was still talking. I remember how John Gay walked back and forth before the fire, me and Boone listening; Alpha and Jolly drinking every word. I recollect things he said: 'They's a world o' dirt flowed under my feet. I never crawled when I was a baby. Just riz up and walked at ten months. I'm a-mind to see every living hill against I die.' "

Grandma wiped her eyes with the hem of her skirt. They watered a bit as she remembered Grandpa. She uncurled her hands before the stove. Hot grease chattered in the skillet. Uncle Jolly caught up a spoonful of corn batter, dropping it into the grease. The boiling fat became as shrill as a flock of starlings.

"Your night-hawking days are over," Uncle Jolly warned. "You're going to stay abed nights if I have to nail the doors."

The fritters were turned; they browned and were stacked high on a plate. And then we sat at the table. We ate the fritters with new poplar-bloom honey; we blew across saucers of black coffee to cool them before drinking.

After breakfast I went to the blacksmith shop to pump the bellows while Uncle Jolly sharpened plowshares. Sunlight leaked through peep cracks in the wall, the room being darksome for all the brightness outside. We hacked and coughed in the dust and coal smoke. The shares yellowed in the furnace bed like the sun blades piercing the cracks. They heated dead white. And how Uncle Jolly smote them on the anvil! He was still angry at Grandma. The hammer rose and fell steady as a clock pendulum. He beat the blades to a hair line. He made them ring like winter axes.

When the shares were done Uncle Jolly made ready to lay-by the corn yonder side Lean Neck. He brought Uncle Luce's horse-mule from the lot. "Fotch a jug o' water along middle o' the morning," he told me, "and keep a watch on Ma. If she starts off, follow."

I couldn't think why he kept worrying about Grandma. He saw my wonder and drew a jaw down, hardly knowing how to tell me this thing. He leaned against Old Bully, hands spread, explaining. "When a body gets old," he began, "they turn chap-like. They're a-liable to get off somewhere and drop stone down dead, only the buzzards seeing where."

I wanted to chop crab grass in the corn. The stalks were in tassel, black-green with growing. Bees worked the tops. Groundhogs fed in daylight in this far patch, and I had in head going to look for their tracks. I might see one sitting on his rump, shucking an ear with his hand-paws.

Uncle Jolly clanged two shares together. "Looky here, feller," he said. "You stay near the house and when I take you to Blackjack we'll go the long way around, Redbird River way. There's a pretty little woman I want to see on Left Fork of Troublesome. We'll make a circle round. We'll go to Troublesome, on to Ball and down, cutting across bloody Breathitt to Leslie County. A sight o' things you'll see on Cutshin, Big Greasy, and Goose Creek. A far piece, but we'll go."

"I'll keep a watch on Grandma," I said, and joy welled inside of me. "I won't go home till they send, a-making." And I thought of Redbird River, and of John Gay who might be walking there, pitching up six pebbly rocks at a time, looking the world over. It would be like going to the scrag end of creation.

Grandma was somewhere in the house, working threads and needles, piecing and patching. I sat under the bubby bush in the yard, my head among the leaves, the boughs clutching my shoulders. It was quiet and warm there. Three ants climbed my leg; they circled my kneebone, touching feelers, and walked down again. A chippy sat on a fence post in the yard, cocking his head. He flew over the bubby bush. Afar in the corn Uncle Jolly sang "Old Talt Hall"—Old Talt Hall killing Frank Salyers; Old Talt Hall sitting in jail writing two letters to his brother: "See your satisfaction, brother. Brother, now farewell." And then he sang "Rich and Rambling Boy."

> I know I am condemned to die,
> And all the girls for me will cry;

But all their cries won't set me free,
For I'm condemned to the gallows-tree.

I shut my eyes and I could see Redbird River flowing green and cool, eddying under the ferns, shaking willow roots; and great forests reached from its banks into the sky. And I thought that if I could see as far for my size as an ant, I could look from the ridgetop and see the river washing through holly thickets; I could see as far as a chippy-bird could fly between daylight and dark. I diddled in my mind. Sunlight sifted through the leaves, slowly, wavering. A bumble bee droned to its nest in the porch sill. I lay down under the bush and slept for a spell.

The morning was half gone when I sat up. I waked, remembering. A jug of water must be carried to Uncle Jolly. By now he would be parched for a drink. The jug had been moved from the spring, so I went into the house to ask Grandma where it was. Grandma would know. She knew in what drawer or what crack a thing was kept; or on what nail it hung. But she wasn't in the kitchen. She was nowhere in the house. I ran to the smokehouse, to the barn, into the garden, calling.

She was gone, and I couldn't think where. Grandma wasn't lost, I knew. I had no fright for her. Uncle Jolly's saying she might drop stone down dead was just to scratch a mark on my memory. But if she walked too far, staying too long, Uncle Jolly wouldn't let me go to Redbird River. "Keep a watch on Ma," he had said. "If she starts off, follow."

Up Lean Neck or down? Over the bench path to Salt Lick and beyond? I looked into the sky, finding not a buzzard saddling blue air. I spat into the frog of my hand, slapping the wet spot with a forefinger. The spit sprang southwest. I set off into the bottom, walking the cowpath along the creek. The path was roofed with brush and vine, and a smell of water was there, a smell of peeled willow, of perch freshly caught. Roots lay on the ground like sunning watersnakes. They had rusty hides, and I stepped carefully. I barely made a track.

I called in the green burrow. Click beetles quieted. A flag blade shook, and was still. A frog grunted under the bank. It was a lonesomy place. And I went on, coming through the wahoo trees into open sunlight. The waters thinned over sandbars, scarcely moving. A snake doctor blew over the surface, searching. I went farther up the creek than I'd ever gone before, past the giant poplars, past the deep hole where Uncle Jolly caught big-mouths. I went pretty near to the second bend.

A thought came into my head and I stopped, listening. Could Grandma have gone to the marking stick?

I called no more. I crept along the path, spying ahead. Turning the second bend I saw the Flaxpatch road wiggling clay ruts toward the creek ford. Elders plagued my sight. I came suddenly upon the marking stick. It was no stick at all; it was a full-grown locust blossoming leaves. It slanted out of the creek where it was first driven. And where it grew Grandpa Middleton had fallen, and his life had hurried like a bird startled on a nest.

Grandma wasn't in sight, and it came to me then where she had gone. She had taken the jug of water to Uncle Jolly herself, not wanting to wake me as I slept under the bubby bush. But I had no time to think of this, for two men came riding from Flaxpatch way. They stood in stirrups as the beasts picked hoofs down steep places. I hid, peeping from the elders. Their faces were strange. One fanned himself with a hat. The horses' flanks were lathery with sweat. And behind them, a little bull of a man came walking. He wore a mine cap with carbide lamp atop. Thick his chest was, and a fleece of black hairs curled out of his shirt.

I stepped from the elders and he spied me. "Be dom," he said, and stopped. "Trying to skeer a feller?" He wiped a sleeve over his face. He took off his cap, and his head was clean as a shaven jaw.

"Now, no," I said. I looked at his double ankles, and his double thumb joints.

"Be dom," he said. "I thought pine-blank you was a mountycat about to spring." He laughed, the flesh of his face catching into a hard knot. "Be dom," he said again, and walked the footlog. In a moment he was gone.

"I bet Walking John Gay never looked odd as that feller," I said to myself. "I never saw John Gay, but I've seen a man strange as ever lived." I thought of how I would tell Uncle Jolly and Grandma about him. I spoke the words aloud to know their sound.

"A feller not five feet high come along, and I skeered him proper. A low-standing feller.

"Oh, he was a little keg of a man, round and thick and double jinted.

"A mountycat he thought I was, fixing to spring.

" 'Be dom,' he kept a-saying."

I would tell of this little fist of a man, never speaking of the locust tree. Never a word of how it grew, tall now and shaggy with leaves.

I turned down the creek, going back the way I had come, going from this death place as from a new grave. I looked back once.

"Brother, now farewell," I said.

I WAKED, my face to the wall, and the pine boards were already yellowed with sunlight. Seven knot holes shaped like dwarf heads looked down on me. From the bed I could reach the resin circles; I could push a forefinger against them until they loosened and fell to the ground outside. Then I'd have to plug them back, for Grandma vowed night air was poisonous, and likely to cause consumption; but I was more afraid of crawlers. A thousand-legged earwig might get inside my head and run me nit-brained. A devil's walking-stick might spit on me. On this morning while studying the knot faces I heard Uncle Jolly shout outside, and Grandma go hurrying into the yard. "Oh, hit must be a sign," Grandma called, "a sign a-flying."

I sprang out of bed. There was no time to jump into my breeches. The thing would have flown by then. I poked out the largest knot and put an eye to it. I saw the thickety slopes of Lean Neck Valley glisten in the morning sun; I saw Uncle Jolly running along the path, peering upward, stumbling, for he did not look at the ground before him. The sky was above, out of my sight. I saw nothing that flew through the air, nor heard a clap or drone of wings. But I heard hoofs coming down Lean Neck. I saw a fat mare and a jinny, with riders atop, taking the long way around to Hardin Town. Two men rode the mare. One straddled the jinny.

In fumbling haste I put on my breeches and hurried into the yard. Grandma was looking toward the corn bottom where Uncle Jolly had gone, paying no mind to the jinny and mare rattling the creek bed road.

"A strange bird a-flying," Grandma explained. "Jolly was bound to take a long look. A bird of a size I never saw before, body big as a dry land goose's, wings spreading as would cover an ax handle, tip to tip. Shroud white all over. Scissor-beaked. Flying low, hit was, searching. Oh, hit was like the roc the Book reads about."

I wanted to run into the corn bottom, to take a look at this queer bird.

"Hit might come back," Grandma said, "or else be gone forever. I don't figure Jolly'll see it agin. Eat your breakfast, child, before it gets stone cold."

I went into the kitchen. A half pone of fatty bread lay on the table, pinched around the edges, and there was a bowl of gravy, brown as a meat skin, to pour over it. The fatty bread crumbled in my plate. I spooned it hastily, hands shaking with excitement.

Grandma poured hot sassafras tea into my cup. She

dropped in a dab of sweetening. "Jolly allus did take
to birds," she said. "When a wee chip of a boy, he'd
point at every one he saw, setting or flying. He kept
the martins scared, forever climbing their poles and
shaking their gourds. Couldn't keep tame pigeons for
him sticking his head in their boxes, a-watching. Recollect once your grandpap killed him a Kentucky redbird. How good tickled Jolly was. Kept that dead
bird in hand allus, slept with it of a night. Maggots got
it finally and Boone had to kill another, swapping without Jolly knowing the differ. He killed five or six,
though it punished him to kill. Boone never favored
killing sport. Never cared a grain for turkey shoots
with fellers taking pot shots, shooting cold. Well, come
a time when he quit that redbird foolishness and gave
Jolly a talking-to.

"'They won't be a bird on the face of the earth the
way folks fire lead around,' he said. 'Hain't right to
take a creature's life just to pleasure yourself. Mighty
nigh like killing folks.' Such a talk-to he gave Jolly,
he's never harmed a bird, never packed a gun for man
nor beast. I'm right proud."

Dew had dried when Uncle Jolly returned. We
were waiting in the yard. He came and stood before
Grandma where she sat on a broken churn amidst the

seasash. His eyes were fierce; his Adam's apple jerked in the nest of his throat as he gulped angrily.

Grandma spoke. "Hit must a-been a reckoning sign for shore." Her voice was almost a whisper, for she saw Uncle Jolly's anger.

"I met three fellers riding down the creek," Uncle Jolly spoke, louder than was need. "They brought damn strange news."

"Son, did you see that there bird-creature agin?"

"I say I got troubling news. Them three come bringing blame."

"Why, nobody went down the creek as I saw."

"Two on a mare, and one on a jenny. That mare swelled fit to bust, and two riding. They'd come across the ridge from Sand Lick, by Aus Coggins' place. Aye, God, Aus claims I cut his fences to giblets four nights ago. Cows got out and et half his crop. One beast died of flounders. Two times now he's blamed me of fence cutting."

"Why, son, I know that hain't so. You've not been off the place for a span."

"My wire cutters are dull as a fro. Hain't been used God knows when. I can prove."

"He won't be asking proof, Aus Coggins won't."

Uncle Jolly blew a stiff breath of wind out of his

chest. His face loosened, and he grinned. "By grab-bies, I hain't too good to cut his fences. I hain't too good, now." His mouth opened, and he began to laugh. "I'd give a war pension to know who done it. I would. It's a fact, I didn't." He glanced at me. "Go fotch the wire cutters, hanging next the harness on the corncrib wall."

"Leave them be," Grandma said. "Aus Coggins's one being I got no pity for. They's a curse on his land. I hear he's got fields won't even grow stickweeds."

"Fotch 'em," Uncle Jolly repeated.

I ran to the barn and searched the corncrib. The rotting leather of Poppet's harness rested on a peg. Mice fled the collar, having built a nest in the straw padding. Around the wall were trace lines, wire stretchers, post-hole diggers, and swingletrees. A de-horner hung with a nail in its mouth. But the wire cut-ters were nowhere to be found.

When I came back without the cutters, neither Uncle Jolly nor Grandma spoke of them. Uncle Jolly was telling about the bird he'd seen. I couldn't get a word in edgewise. "That flier's throat was like a crook-neck gourd, hit's head cocked one-sided. Legs long and thin, and stickweedy. A crane-bird, I reckon. Lost, and hunting its way back to where it come from."

"The cutters are gone," I said.

"Listen, child," Grandma spoke impatiently.

"I run after till it flew beyond sight," Uncle Jolly went on. "Then I come on them fellers riding down-creek. One on a jinny. Two on a mare, and her in a bearing way. Liable to drop a colt any time. A shame, and I spoke it. Mad through I was anyhow for the blame they brought, and I cussed all three to a fare-you-well."

"I allus wanted me a colt," I said. "I allus did."

"I said to them dobbers: 'Come your next trip, bring an eye witness to settle your lies. And tell Aus Coggins to stand clear, or I'll give him something regular to grunt about. He's already drawed more breath than's his due."

"I allus did long for a colt," I said.

THE pawpaws got ripe in early October while Uncle Jolly laid out a two-week spell in the county jail for roughing Les Honeycutt at a box supper on Left Troublesome. Uncle Toll rode over to Hardin Town on Old Bully, taking the word Grandma sent. I went along, riding behind Uncle Toll, carrying three pawpaws in a poke. They were fat ones, black and rotten-ripe, smelling sweeter than a bubby bush. We reached the head of Big John Riggins Creek by noon. It made us hungry to smell the poke.

"How many paws you got there?" Uncle Toll asked. I said: "Three," and Uncle Toll said he reckoned we ought to eat one apiece, saving the greenest for Uncle Jolly. "The greenest will be the keepingest," he said.

I picked the smallest, and the tender skin came half off in my hand, the sticky juice oozing out of the yellow flesh. Uncle Toll popped it into his mouth, blowing the big seeds over the animal's bony head.

"I know a feller's name puts me in mind o' pawpaws," I said. "Hit's Fruit Corbitt."

"Hain't you eating one?" Uncle Toll asked.

"I'd be nigh ashamed to take Uncle Jolly just one

paw," I said. "One just calls for another. If'n I got
started, it would take a bushel to dull the edge on my
tongue. Anyhow, I like 'em better when they've had a
touch o' frost."

"Hain't no use taking that sorry Jolly a grain o'
nothing," Uncle Toll said. "I figure he gets along
pearter on jail cooking than anything else. He's et
a-plenty. Two years he got in the state pen for dinnymiting Pate Horn's mill dam, and after he'd been shet
up nine months they give him a parole. Now he's fit
and cracked two o' Les Honeycutt's rib bones, and
them Honeycutts might make a sight o' trouble. It's
not beyond thinking they'll fotch him back to Frankfort."

"Uncle Jolly fit him fair," I said. "I heard Les cut
the saddle off his nag. No man a-living would a-tuck
that."

Uncle Toll drew the reins tight in his hands and
we set off faster down the crusty road.

"Jolly was sparking Les's sweetheart," Uncle Toll
said, his words louder and a little edgy. "Trying to
make up to Bowlegs Sawyers's daughter, Tina. I don't
lay a blame on Les. They's a lot o' things bigger'n
eyes and ears you never seed nor heard tell of."

We went on, not speaking until the wheel-deepened
road crawled over the ridge into the head of Trouble-

some Creek. We stopped where the waters drained out of a bog, spring-clear and cold. Uncle Toll got off the horse-mule and let him drink, and I slid to the ground. Bully drank his fill. Uncle Toll tied him to the muscled limb of a hornbeam, and we scooped water in our hats.

"You can set in the saddle a spell," Uncle Toll said, when we were ready to go. He swung me up, pulling himself behind, and we went down the trace of waters into the valley. The horse-mule swung his head nervously, crowding against the ditch growth. Uncle Toll kept reaching for the reins, jerking him back into the road.

"Hit's a pity you can't hold him out o' the blackberry vines," he said. "If this keeps on, I won't have a stitch o' breeches against we reach Hardin Town. These here briers are raveling them out, string at a time."

At the creek's fork we turned into Hardin Town, hitching the horse-mule to a locust post before the courthouse. Uncle Jolly saw us coming and shouted out to us, his face tight between the window bars. Logg Turner opened the jailhouse door. We went into a stone-damp hall, Logg fumbling through his long keys for one to Uncle Jolly's cell.

"I could nigh open it with my eyeteeth before you

picked the key," Uncle Jolly said, twisting his mouth like Logg's.

We went into the cell, the door catching itself back on rusty hinges. Uncle Jolly grabbed me by the arms, swinging me around twice, scraping my heels on the walls. "Big enough in here to swing a fox by its tail," he said. He dropped me atop a quilt-ball on his cot and shook Uncle Toll's hand until the knuckles cracked.

"Hain't no use breaking a feller's arm off," Uncle Toll said.

Logg rattled his keys and grinned at us. Jolly winked at him, making a sly pass at the keys and tipping them with his fingers. Logg jerked the iron ring back, quickly though not uneasily, knowing Uncle Jolly's ways.

"Fotch some chairs for us to set on," Uncle Jolly said. "Hain't you got no manners a-tall?"

Logg showed his stumpy teeth. "Fotch 'em yourself," he said. "They's a bench setting just outside the cell." He went up the hall, leaving the door open, and Uncle Jolly dragged the whittled seat in.

"Logg's mighty feisty, for election time to be so nigh," Uncle Jolly said.

"It's a tall risk not locking that door," Uncle Toll said.

"I hain't going nowheres," Uncle Jolly laughed. "Next rusty I cut, it's the pen two years for shore."

"Ma sent me to say what you've spoke," Uncle Toll said. "She never reckoned you'd have sense to know."

"This is my pigeon roost," Uncle Jolly said. "I nest right natural in jail, and it's a fact. I get lonesome sometimes, though, nigh enough to start figuring a way out. Reckon I can't trust myself to stay locked in long. Nobody here but me now. The sheriff turned everybody loose to pull corn. They won't be finishing their spells till after gathering."

"You just got nine days more," Uncle Toll counted. "Looks to me you could nail yourself here till then, but I wouldn't trust you spitting distance. Two breaks you've made out o' this jail times past."

"If I had me somebody to talk to," Uncle Jolly said, "I'd fare well."

"Logg ought to be a heap o' company."

"Ruther hear a bull frog croaking."

"Nine days hain't long—one Sunday and eight weekdays."

"I'm liable to scratch out before then."

"That's fool talk. They'll salt you in Frankfort for shore."

"Wouldn't pitch a straw for the differ."

Pawpaw scent lay heavy in the room, pushing down

the mullein-rank jail smells. Uncle Jolly looked at the poke in my hand. "If I was a 'possum," he said, "I wouldn't know better what you got."

I drew out the pawpaws, holding them toward him. "A good frosting would make them a sight better," I said.

"Take just one," Uncle Toll told Uncle Jolly. "He hain't et since we left home."

Uncle Jolly picked the smaller, though I held the fat one closer. He pitched it toward the ceiling and let it fall into his open mouth. The seeds popped forth, shot across the room and between the bars into the yard, touching nothing. "You couldn't do that if your life and neck was strung on it," he said. I tried with my seeds, blowing them hard, but they fell to the floor. Uncle Jolly kicked them under the bed and went into the hall, calling to Logg. "Have you got any o' them biled shucks left?"

We spooned the beans Logg brought, coated with grease, and as good eating as anything on this earth. They were good to bite into, tender and juicy. I could have eaten more, but I did not speak of it, thinking Logg had scraped the pot.

"I hain't got nothing agin jail victuals," Uncle Jolly said. "They come regular as clock-tick, three times a day."

"If your belly's content, there's no cause to snake out before your time is up," Uncle Toll argued. "Your ma sent on word for you to stay."

"If I had me somebody to talk to, it wouldn't be so bran-fired eternal. All I do is set and set, and then set some more."

The horse-mule whinnied in the yard. Uncle Toll looked out, getting uneasy and ready to go. "Sun-ball's drapping fast," he said. "Four hours' ride 'twixt here and home. Ought to be a-going. Ma told me to fotch back a ten-pound o' salt and I got to roust that."

"Set yourself down," Uncle Jolly commanded. "I hain't got my talk through."

Uncle Toll walked across the room. He looked at me and cocked his head. "Reckon you could stay here nine days?" he asked.

"This here's no place for a chap," Uncle Jolly said. "Anyhow, it's time he headed back to his folks at Blackjack. One solid year he has been away."

"He'd be a sight o' company. I figure you'd hang around yourself if he was here. And nine days coming you can fotch him to the camps."

"Hit's agin the law for a chap to stay shet in jail, but Logg gets right free when he's needing votes. He could put a cot and chair in the hall, and that wouldn't be in jail nor out."

"Getting late," Uncle Toll complained. "I'll talk to Logg, and mosey along. I figure Logg'll let me have my way. My vote is good as the next 'un."

Logg said I could stay. I wanted to, though I knew first frost would come any morning now, and I would miss my fill of pawpaws. They were best after a killing frost, mushy and sweet, falling apart almost at the touch.

When Uncle Toll was ready to go, I went into the yard to see him off. He rode away, the horse-mule walking swiftly toward the forks with his great bones sticking out hard and sharp. Uncle Jolly leaned against the window bars and called down. "First time I ever seed a feller straddling a quilting frame."

With election time near, the county seat was filled with people, their mounts chocking stiff heels in the courthouse yard. Before daylight, horses came sloshing through the creek, setting hoofs carefully into dark waters.

"Candidates thicker'n groundhogs in a roast-ear patch," Logg told us. "Got where a feller can't go down the road peaceable."

"Bet you argue as many votes as the next 'un," Uncle Jolly said.

"I don't worry a man's years off."

"You'd vote your ol' nag and jinny if they was registered."

"I get a vote any way can be got, buy or swap, hog-back or straddle-pole, but when they're drapped in the ballot box, I allus say: 'Boys, count 'em square and honest.' "

Two days before Uncle Jolly's time was up, Logg came hurrying from the courthouse. He came with his keys jingling on his belt, and we heard him coming afar.

"I seen Les Honeycutt talking to Judge Mauldin," Logg said. "I figger he's trying to get you sent back to Frankfort. Les's folks can swing nigh every vote on Jones Fork, and the judge knows it. He can't be re-elected with the Honeycutts agin him."

"I never pushed Les's ribs in fur enough," Uncle Jolly said. "I reckon the judge hain't going to give plumb over. He'll be needing a few Baldridge and Middleton votes on Little Carr and Defeated Creek. That Les Honeycutt ought to have his long nose trimmed and pickled in vinegar. He hain't got a chance o' locking me away from Tina Sawyers. You can't lock bees from a honeycomb."

It was dark inside the jail when Judge Mauldin rat-tled the iron door, though light held outside. Night chill had settled into the wall stones, and there was a hint of frost in the air. He came in, rubbing his fat hands. Logg opened Uncle Jolly's cell and I followed, going close behind Logg. Judge Mauldin sat down heavily on the cot, twisting his watch chain around a thick finger. There was a bushtail squirrel carved from a peach seed hanging on the chain's end, real as life.

"Reckon you heard the Honeycutts are trying to hog-tie me into sending you back to Frankfort," the judge said.

"I heard a little sketch," Uncle Jolly said, threading his arms through the bars.

The judge groaned. "I can't spare a vote."

"You'll lose a mess either way," Uncle Jolly warned. "I got no notion o' going back to the pen anyhow. A log team couldn't drag me there agin. It's like pulling eyeteeth just to stay in this jailhouse."

Logg brought in a smoky lantern, holding a match to the oily wick.

The judge cracked heavy knuckles against his palms. "I'm not a-going to send you back," he said. "I got it figured this way. You stay in jail till election day— then it won't matter who rows up. I just want me one more term. Logg'll loose you the minute the Honeycutts get voted on Jones Fork."

"That's eight days a-coming," Uncle Jolly said. "It'll keep me here plumb till hog-killing time. Like setting on a frog gig staying, and me knowing I could snake out any time the notion struck."

"You've gone nowhere yet, as I see," Logg said.

Uncle Jolly looked at the ring of keys hung on Logg's belt. "Never took a strong idea," he said. "I hain't safe in here long as there's a key walking around. I can't trust myself to stay shet up."

"If you don't stay, I'll be bound to send you back to Frankfort," Judge Mauldin warned.

The judge stood to go. I went out behind him, Logg following and locking the door, and hooking the ring on his belt. Uncle Jolly thrust his arms through the bars as Logg turned, lifting the ring with a finger, quick as an eye-bat. I glimpsed it all and waited, holding my breath, fearing for Uncle Jolly. The judge and Logg walked up the hall, not looking back or knowing. When they had gone, Uncle Jolly took one key off, handing the rest to me. "Go take the others back," he said. "This one won't be missed for a spell."

I went to bed early, for there was no heat in the cold hallway. In the night I waked, thinking someone had spoken. Uncle Jolly had called, speaking my name into pitch dark. His words were barely louder than the straw ticking rustling in my ears. I stepped on the stone floor, feeling my way to the cell. Uncle Jolly was there, though I couldn't see him. He reached through the bars and found my hand, putting the stolen key into it.

"You go home at the crack o' day and get a wad o' dirt betwixt us before Logg misses it," he said. "Give the key to your grandma and tell her to keep it eight days, and then have it fotched back—eight days and not a minute yon side. Tell her I said it."

I felt my way along the wall, crawling back into the warm spot in my bed, and slept until the morning slosh of horses' feet in the creek awakened me.

Logg opened the jailhouse door for me when light broke. The steps were moldy white. The season's first frost lay on the ground. "Hit's a killer," Logg said. "This here one ought to make the shoats squeal." I set off, walking fast over the frosted road, knowing the pawpaws were fat and winter-ripe on Lean Neck ridge.

III

THE hail of early June shredded the growing blades of corn, and a windstorm breaking over Little Angus Creek in July flattened the sloping fields; but the hardy stalks rose in the hot sun, and the fat ears fruited and ripened. The mines at Blackjack had closed again and Father had rented a farm that spring on the hills rising from the mouth of Flaxpatch on Little Angus. We moved there during a March freeze, and the baby died that week of croup. When sap lifted in sassafras and sourwood, Father sprouted the bush-grown patches, and plowed deep with a mule Quin Adams lent him. With corn breaking through the furrows and the garden seeded, he left us to tend the crop, going over in Breathitt County to split rock in Mace Hogan's quarry. There was good seasoning in the ground. Shucks bulged on heavy corn ears. Garden furrows were cracked where potatoes pushed the earth outward in their growing.

Weeds plagued the corn, and Mother took us to the fields. We were there at daylight, chopping horsemint and crab grass with blunt hoes. Sister Euly could trash us all with a corn row. She was growing beanpole-tall, and thin and quick like Mother. Fletch had grown during the summer. His face was round as a butter ball. He dug too deep, often missing the weeds and cutting the corn. Mother let him take the short rows. He slept during hot afternoons at the field's edge, deep in a patch of tansy with bees worrying dusty blossoms over his head.

"Hit's a sight to have such a passel of victuals after living tight as a tow-wad," Mother said. "If Saul Highnight hadn't laid claim to the heifer, we'd had milk and butter too. The baby might o' lived." Mother cried while telling about the heifer. "He heard the calf was alive and sent a man to fotch it. He was ashamed to come a-claiming himself."

We raised thirty-six dommers. They scarcely pecked at the bran we threw out, for there was such a plenty of food in the fields and patches. You could holler "chickeroo" the day long and they wouldn't come.

Tomatoes ripened faster than could be canned. The old apple trees in the bottom were burdened. We peeled and sulphured three bushels of McIntoshes. Fall beans were strung and hung with peppers and onions on the porch. The cushaws were a wonder to see, bloated with yellow flesh. The crook-neck gourds on the lot fence grew too large for water dippers. They were just right to hang on martin poles.

"If we stay on here, I'm going to have me a mess o' martins living in them gourds," I told Mother.

"We'll just settle down awhile if your poppy is a-mind to," Mother said. "A sight the rations we've got."

With the crops laid by, we cleared a patch of ground on the Point around the baby's grave. Mother took up a bucket of white sand from the Flaxpatch sandbar, patting it on the mound with her hands. "We're going to have a funeralizing for the baby in September," she said. "Your poppy will be agin it, but we're going to, whether or no. I've already spoke for Brother Sim Mobberly. He's coming all the way from Troublesome Creek. I reckon we've got plenty to feed everybody."

There was nothing more to do in the garden and fields, and during this first rest since spring Mother began to grieve over the baby. Euly told us that she cried in the night. We spoke quietly. There was no noise in the house. The bottle-flies on the windows and katydids outside sang above our speaking. With Mother suddenly on edge, and likely to cry at a word, we played all day on the hills. Euly ran about the coves like a young fox, coming in before supper with a poke of chestnuts and chinquapins. I found her playhouse once in a haw patch. Eight corncob poppets sat on rock chairs, eating giblets of cress from mud dishes. I skittered away, Euly never knowing I had been near.

Fletch followed me everywhere, forever wanting to go where I went. Sometimes I hid, choosing to play by myself, and talk things aloud, but he would call until his voice hoarsened and trembled. Then I was ashamed not to answer, and I'd pretend I had just come into hollering distance. He would run to me, dodging through the weeds like a puppy. There was no getting away from Fletch. We fished dirt holes for johnny-humpbacks. If I caught one first he spat down the hole for spite. Oft we would tale-tell. I told about Uncle Toll's finger-piece, Walking John Gay, and the pigeon-birds; and of my going to Redbird River. "Tell agin you going to Redbird," Fletch would say. So many times I had told I knew the words by heart. "Uncle Jolly brought me home the far way round," I would begin. "First he went a-sparking Tina Sawyers on Left Troublesome, then we struck toward Redbird River country. I saw Cutshin and Goose Creek, Big Greasy and Hoss Neck. And Redbird was the biggest waters a-tall, clear as goblet-glass. I saw things Walking John Gay went many a mile to see. I saw country like a dream dreamt. . . ."

Oft we talked of growing up, of what we were going to do then. "When I'm growed to a man," I'd brag,

"I figger to be a horse doctor. Hain't going to be a
miner, buried down like a johnny-humpback." Fletch
thought he wanted to be a horse doctor too. "Me," he
would say, "I hain't a-going to be a miner neither."

One day Fletch and I came in from the buckeye
thicket with our pockets loaded. Mother and Euly
were working around a dead willow in the yard, stringing the twigless branches with saved eggshells. The
eggs had been broken carefully at each end, letting
the whites and yolks run out. The little tree was about
five feet high, and the lean branches were already
nearly covered with shells.

"I allus did want me an egg tree," Mother said. "I
hear tell it's healthy to have one growing in the yard.
And I figure it'll be brightening to the house. A sight o'
folks will be coming to the funeralizing. My dommers
ought to lay nigh enough to kiver the last branch before the time. Eggshells hain't a grain o' good except to
prettify with."

August lay heavy on the fields when Father came
home for three days. Blooming whitetop covered the
pasture before the house, and spindling stickweeds
shook out purple bonnets. Father came just before
dark, and the pretty-by-nights were open and peart by
the doorsill. He trudged into the yard without seeing

the egg tree, or the blossoms beside the steps. He walked up on the porch, and we saw his red nose and watery eyes. Mother caught him by the arm.

"Hit's this plagued hay fever," Father said. "Every bloom on the face o' the earth is giving off dust. Sometimes it nigh chokes me black in the face."

He sniffled, blew his nose, and went inside with Mother. His angry voice suddenly filled the house. Mother brought out an armload of yellowrods, stickweed blooms, and farewell-summer Euly had stuck around in fruit jars.

Father's face darkened when Mother told him about the funeralizing for the baby. "I've already sent on word to Brother Sim Mobberly," she said.

Father groaned. "It's onreckoning what a woman'll think about with her man off trying to make a living," he said. "Green hadn't even larnt to walk. There hain't any use for a big funeral."

"We've got plenty to feed everybody," Mother said. "I ain't ashamed of what we got. We've done right proud this year. I'm just getting one preacher, and it's going to be a one-day funeral."

"There hain't no use asking anybody except our kin," Father said. "It'll look like we're trying to put on the dog."

"Everybody that's a-mind to come is asked,"

Mother said. "I hain't trying to put a peck measure over the word o' God."

Father got up and lighted the rio lamp. "We'll feed right good down at Blackjack this winter," he said. "I hear tell the mines are to open the middle of October—this time for good. I'm going back to Mace Hogan's quarry for another two weeks and then I'm quitting. I'm longing to git me a pick and stick it in a coal vein. I can't draw a clean breath of air outside a mine this time o' year. It's like a horse trying to breathe with his nose in a meal poke."

"I was reckoning we'd stay on here another crap," Mother said. "The mines is everly opening and closing. I been told there's no school in Blackjack this fall. The baby is buried here. Oh, I never favored bringing up my children in a coal camp. They've got enough meanness in their blood without humoring it. We done right well crapping this year. We raised a passel of victuals."

"Going to be good times agin in Blackjack," Father said. "I hear they're to pay nigh fifty cents a ton for coal loading. And they're building some new company houses. I got my word in for one."

Mother's face was pale in the lamplight. "I reckon it's my egg tree I'm hating to leave," she said. "I allus did want me one."

"Fresh news to me," Father said. "I hain't seen one

since before I married and was traipsing round in Buck-
horn Creek. I wisht all the timber was egg trees. They
don't give off a grain o' dust. This Little Angus hollow
is dusty as a pea threshing. It nigh makes a feller
sneeze his lungs out."

"I'm a-mind to stay on here," Mother said, her voice
chilled and tight. "It's the nighest heaven I've been on
this earth."

Fall came in the almanac, and the sourwood bushes
were like fire on the mountains. Leaves hung bright and
jaundiced on the maples. Red foxes came down the
hills, prowling outside our chicken house, and hens
squalled in the night. Quin Adams's hounds hunted
the ridges, their bellies thin as saw blades. Their voices
came bellowing in the dark hours. Once, waking suddenly, I heard a fox bark defeat somewhere in the cove
beyond Flaxpatch.

Mother had set the funeralizing for the last Sunday
in September. Father came on the Wednesday before,
bringing a headstone split from Mace Hogan's quarry.
It was solid limerock. The baby's name had been
carved on one side with a chisel. We took it to the
Point, standing it at the head of the mound. Father
built an arbor there of split poplar logs. We thatched
the roof with linn branches.

"It's big enough for Brother Sim to swing his arms without hitting anybody," Father said.

Mother climbed the hill to see it. "I wisht to God I'd had a picture tuck of the baby so it could be sot in the arbor during the meeting. I wisht to God I'd had it tuck."

Father felled locusts, laying the trunks in front of the arbor for seats, and Mother took a pair of mule shears, cutting the weeds and grass evenly.

Uncle Jolly came Thursday morning. He came a-straddle a dwarf pony. His feet nearly dragged dirt. He came singing at the top of his voice:

> Polish my boots
> And set 'em on the bench,
> Going down to Jellico
> To see Rafe Shanks.
> Holler-ding, baby, holler-ding.
>
> Ol' gray goose went to the river,
> If'n I'd been a gander
> I'd went thar with 'er.
> Holler-ding, baby, holler-ding.

When he turned over the Little Angus sandbar, Uncle Jolly crossed his legs in the saddle, and came riding the yard path, right onto the porch, and would have gone pony and all into the house if Mother hadn't been standing in the door. Father laughed, saying: "Jolly allus was a damned fool," and Uncle Jolly got so tickled he reeled on the porch, holding his stomach, and fell into the pretty-by-night bed.

"Where's Ma?" Mother inquired. "I wanted most for her to come."

Uncle Jolly rose among the blossoms, playing like one leg was shorter than the other. "Ma's puny," he said. "Didn't feel well enough to take the trip. Said for me to come on, and to tell you all she wasn't going to live eternal and forever, and for all to come to see her. I got Elias Horn's woman to stay with her till I get back. And I borrowed Elias's pony-devil to ride."

"I've been aiming to go," Mother said. "I had in head going the first chance."

Uncle Jolly looked toward the far end of the yard. "By juckers," he said. "First tree ever I saw lay eggs."

Aunt Rilla and Uncle Luce came in time for dinner, walking the creek bed road with Lala, Crilla, Tishy, and Lue strung out behind. Aunt Rilla carried Foan, the youngest, in her arms. Nezzie Crouch came walking alone from Blackjack, tired from the eleven-mile journey. Uncle Toll and Aunt Sue Ella were there by daylight next morning, and we all set to work getting ready for Sunday. The floors were scrubbed twice over with a shuck mop, and the smoky walls washed down.

Jimson-weeds were cut in the backyard; the woodpile
was straightened. Mother cut the heads off of fifteen
dommers and our last guinea. The stove stayed hot all
day Friday, baking and frying. Cushaw pies covered
the kitchen table.

"I reckon you've got enough shucky beans biled to
feed creation," Nezzie Crouch said. "Alpha, you hain't
never been in such a good fix. You'd be puore foolish
moving to Blackjack agin. Hit's been a hard scrabble
there."

"Since I married I've been driv from one coal camp
to another," Mother said, taking her hands out of
bread dough. "I've lived hard as nails. I've lived at Blue
Diamond. I've lived at Chavies, Tribbey, Butterfly
Two, Elkhorn, and Lackey. We moved to Hardburly
twice, and to Blackjack beyond counting. I reckon I've
lived everywhere on God's green earth. Now I want
to set me down and rest. The baby is buried here, and
I've earnt a breathing spell. We done right well this
crap. We got plenty."

Aunt Sue Ella kept us children shooed out of the
kitchen. We hung around Uncle Jolly until he put a
lizard up Fletch's breeches leg, and threw a bucket of
water on the rest of us. "Sometimes I fair think Jolly
is a witty," Aunt Rilla said.

Father met Preacher Sim Mobberly at the mouth of

Flaxpatch Saturday morning, taking Elias Horn's nag for him to ride. But they both came back walking, being ashamed to straddle the sorry mount. Father said he didn't know the pony had a saddle boil until he had started with her.

Preacher Sim slept on the feather bed that night. Father took the men out to the barn to sleep on the hay. Aunt Rilla and Aunt Sue Ella took Mother's bed, the rest of us sleeping on pallets spread upon the floor.

The moon was full, and big and shiny as a brass pot. It was daywhite outside. I couldn't sleep, feeling the strangeness of so many people in the house, and the unfamiliar breathing. Before day I went to the corn-crib and got a nap until the rooster crowed, not minding the mice rustling the shucks in the feed basket.

Mother climbed to the Point before breakfast to spread a white sheet over the baby's grave. When she came down the Adamses were there, Quin looking pale with his first shave of the fall, and Mrs. Adams flushed and hot, not wanting to sit down and wrinkle her starched dress. Cleve Cockerel and his family were not far behind. The Gearhards, the Letchers, the Ootens came; folk were there from Dans Fork, Hurricane Branch, Rowdy, Old Trace, Pushback Hollow, Saw Pit.

Before nine o'clock the yard and porch were

crowded. Neighbors came quietly, greeting Mother, and the women held handkerchiefs in their hands, crying a little. Then we knew again that there had been death in our house. All who went inside spoke in whispers, their voices having more words than sound. The clock was stopped, its hands pointing to the hour and minute the baby died; and those who passed through the room knew the bed, for it was spread with a white counterpane and a bundle of fall roses rested upon it.

At ten o'clock Preacher Sim opened his Bible in the arbor on the Point. "Oh, my good brethren," he said, stroking his white beard, "we was borned in sin, and saved by grace." He spat upon the ground, and lifted his hands toward the withered linn thatching. "We have come together to ask the blessed Saviour one thing pine-blank. Can a little child enter the Kingdom of Heaven?"

The leaves came down. October's frost stiffened the brittle grass, and spiders' webs were threads of ice in the morning sun. We gathered corn during the cool days, sledding it down the snaky trail to the barn. Pigs came out of the hills from mast hunting and rooted up bare potato rows with damp snouts. Father went to Blackjack and stayed a week. When he returned there was coal dust ground into the flesh of his hands. He had worked four days in the mines.

"I promised to get moved in three days," Father said. "We got a new house waiting, with two windows in every room."

"I'm a-longing to stay on here," Mother said. Her voice was small and hoping. "I'll be staying with the children, and you can go along till spring. Moving hain't nothing but leaving things behind."

Father cracked his shoes together in anger. "That's clear foolishness you're speaking," he said, reddening. "I hain't aiming to be a widow-man this year."

"I'm sot agin moving," Mother said, "but I reckon I'm bound to. If we could stop by Lean Neck and see Ma though, I'd take more satisfaction going."

"We ought to be moving by Thursday," Father said. "No sense dragging our stuff eighteen miles out o' the way. Come spring, you can go see your ma."

"Nigh we get our roots planted, we keep pulling them up and planting in furrin ground," Mother complained. "Moving is an abomination. Thar's a sight of things I hate to leave here. I hate to leave my egg tree I set so much time and patience on. Reckon it's my egg tree holding me."

"I never heered tell o' such foolishness," Father said. "Pity thar hain't a seed so it can be planted agin."

Cold rains came over the Angus hills, softening the roads and deepening wheel tracks. There could be no moving for a spell, though Father was anxious to be loading the wagon. Mother sat before the fire, making no effort to pack, while rain fell through the long, slow days.

"Rain hain't never lost a day for a miner," Father said, walking the floor restlessly.

"You ought to be nailing together a little covering for the baby's grave then," Mother said. Father fetched walnut planks from the loft and built a gravehouse under the barn shed. It was five feet square with a chestnut shingle roof. During the first lull in the weather, we took it to the Point.

When the rain stopped, fog hung in the coves, and the hills were dark and weather-gray. Cornstalks stood awkwardly unbalanced in the fields. The trees looked sodden and dead, and taller than when in leaf. Father took our stove down one night. The next morning the mule was hitched to the wagon, and the hind gate lowered before the back door. Mother gave us a cold baked potato for breakfast, then began to pack the dishes. We were on Flaxpatch road by eight o'clock, Mother sitting on the jolt-seat beside Father, and looking back toward the Point where the gravehouse stood among bare locusts.

We reached Blackjack in middle afternoon. The slag pile towering over the camp burned with an acre of oily flames. A sooty mist hung over the creek bottom. Our house sat close against a bare hill. It was cold and gloomy, smelling sourly of paint, but there were glass windows, and Euly, Fletch, and I ran into every room to look out.

A pied cat came to smell the meat box. Old neighbors dropped in to shake our hands and to stare at the dried, pickled, and canned victuals we had brought; and then went away. Nezzie Crouch stayed to help. She tried to scare the pied cat, but he would not be frightened. "Jist a gypsy cat," she said, "bad to take up with newcomers. Folks call him Ol' Bartow."

Father started back after the last load as soon as the wagon was empty, leaving us to set the beds. He came back in the dark of the morning, none of us hearing him enter the gate.

We were awake at daybreak, feeling the nakedness of living in a house with many windows. We went on the porch and looked up the rutted road. Men walked the mud with carbide lamps burning on their caps. Mother came out presently and we went into the yard with her. There was the egg tree. Its roots were buried shallowly in damp earth near the fence corner. Some of the shells were cracked, and others had fallen off, exposing brown willow branches. Mother turned and went back into the house. "It takes a man-person to be a puore fool," she said.

I T was middle afternoon. Euly and I ran along the road to see the town, and to look into the creek beyond. We stole away from Fletch. I had in head seeing the two blind mules Father had told me the foreman kept at his place. We looked at the rows of houses in the valley bottom. Eight houses were high on the hill. At the far end of the camp rooms hung over creek waters, sitting on posts. Our homeseat was near the burning slag pile, low in a nest of houses. The camp was alive with the groan of the coal conveyor. It rang through the town like a rusty bell.

"I used to know who lived in every house," Euly said, "but a pack of strangers have moved in. I hardly know a body."

"Recollect the feller who grabbled a mole in our garden?" I asked. "Sid Pindler, his name was. Ab Stevall and Fruit Corbitt come with him. If'n I met air one, I'd know 'em."

"Fruit is the storekeeper," Euly said. "Once I went to buy a box o' pepper and he dropped a piece of horehound candy in the poke."

We walked a wheel-rut, deep as the mouths of our shoes. Women passed, coming from the storehouse with brown pokes resting on their arms. A smell of salt meat and water-ground meal hung after them.

"I hear they's a fortune-telling woman lives in this camp," Euly said. "I'd give anything to have my fortune told."

"An herb doc lives here," I reminded. "Recollect Nezzie Crouch said so. Wonder if they's a granny woman?"

"We're going to buy buttermilk from Nezzie Crouch," Euly bragged, "and I'm going to fotch it every day."

A man came down the road carrying a small rooster. He held the fowl's legs firmly between forefinger and thumb, a hand resting on its back. The rooster was fairly hidden in his arm-crotch. We looked after him. "Where, now, can he be a-going with that banty?" I asked. Euly shook her head, not knowing. "He might be a furriner," she said. "He's not got our look-like. I bet he was born afar yonder in West Virginia."

We stopped, listening. Doors opened and shut, knobs rattled. Thumb-latches clicked. Feet trod the floors. Children came into the road to toss stocking balls, pitching them back and forth. A ball was missed, rolling at my feet. I picked it up, bending my arm to throw. The boy waited, not lifting his hands for the catch, watching me. I threw it back. He let the ball strike the ground, roll, and die. He caught it up and went into the house without looking back. A face was pressed against a smoky window, and withdrawn.

A man came walking, his corduroy breeches rustling. He wore three shirts, one atop another, and there were three collars leafed about his neck. A ball was tossed to him and he bounced it on the ground, skipping like a boy. The children laughed. They grabbed at his coat pockets, reaching into them, pulling. They drew forth bits of string and bright paper, and shiny tobacco tags. His pockets were turned wrongside out and the children scrambled upon the ground for the falling pretties. A baby-child toddled between the man's spread legs, screaming with joy. The man hopped on one foot, spun on a heel, and laughed.

"He's Jace Haggin," Euly said, cupping her words into a whisper. "Ol' Reece Haggin's son. I saw him when we lived in Blackjack last time. He's a man not growed up in his mind."

"He's got three shirts on," I said. "I bet he's rich."

"Now, no," Euly said. "He's a born witty, and don't know better than to carry all his clothes on his back."

"Hit's a pity-sake," I said.

Jace Haggin came up to us. He stood gentle as a shep

dog. He held out three hand-made tops. "Want to play spinny?" he asked. "Want to?"

"We're going to spy in the creek and see if they's fish," Euly answered.

"I was going to see the foreman's blind mules if'n I found out where he lived," I said.

Euly frowned, for I had not told her about the mules.

Jace put the tops into his pocket. We watched him, restless to be going, treading the ground with our feet. We were a bit afraid.

"Darb Sorrels lives a full mile upcreek," Jace said.

We began to move, heads over shoulders. We ran. We ran all the way to the creek.

"I saw a strange feller once," I said, looking into the water. "Hit was on Lean Neck, and a little bull of a man come along, and him not got a hair on topside of his head. 'Be dom,' he kept a-saying."

The waters ran yellow, draining acid from the mines, cankering rocks in its bed. The rocks were snuffy brown, eaten and crumbly. There were no fishes swimming the eddies, nor striders looking at themselves in the waterglass. Bare willows leaned over. They threw a golden shadow on the water.

"Going to see them mules was a lie-tale," Euly said spitefully.

"Hope me to die," I swore. "Hit's truth. I'd go straight if I knew the way." I looked into the water and thought of myself riding a little mule, my feet swinging in the stirrups. A mule my very own. How proudly I rode in my mind; Father, Mother, and Euly watching, and Fletch stubbed with envy. "Come the chance, I'm going to ride one o' them mules," I said. I grew bold. I spoke out. "I hain't going to be a miner when I grow to a man, a-breathing bug-dust inside a hill. I aim to be a horse doctor. I am, now."

Suddenly the metal groan of the coal conveyor stopped. The camp was hollow with quiet. Then we heard a shout, a man's halloo. It came from the drift-mouth. Feet began to thump the paths curling into the road. Empty dinner buckets rattled. Doors swung wide and women and children came out on the porches. The smell of frying meat came with them.

"It's men coming from the mines," Euly said.

Miners tramped the road, walking four abreast. They came with lamps burning, their heads bobbing, and with faces smudged.

We leapt forward. We raced toward our house, wanting to get home before Father arrived. Euly held back, letting me keep up, for she was swifter. We went into our house through the back door, and there was Uncle Samp come to stay a spell with us.

"A FAIR place you've got here," Uncle Samp said. He sat in the kitchen after supper, under the white bloom of the rio lamps, his chair leaned against the wall. His eyes rounded, looking. Three fly-bugs walked stupidly across the ceiling, wings tight against their bodies, drunk with light. Euly peered through the window into the dark. Fletch crawled around the table, pushing a match box, playing it was a coal gon. Old Bartow followed Fletch, snatching playfully at his breeches legs. "Never you lived in such a bran-fired new house as I've got reckoning of," Uncle Samp said. "Aye, gonnies, if there hain't windows looking four directions." He tipped the blunt end of his mustache with a thumb. It was a knuckle-joint long now, combed stiff and thin, the hairs as coarse as a boar's whiskers.

"Camp houses setting on three sides and hills blacking the other," Mother said. "Can't see a thing beyond." Her words were dolesome, though not complaining. She glanced at Uncle Samp as she dried the dishpan, and Father looked too from where he sat beside the stove. A thready web of veins was bright on Uncle Samp's cheeks. His hands rested on his knees, fat and tender, and they had none of the leathery look of a miner's. I remembered then what Mother had said to Father before supper, whispering in the kitchen while Uncle Samp napped in the far room.

"Fifty years old if he's a day," she had said, "and never done a day's work. A man of his years ought to be married, keeping his own. A shame he'll put up on his kin when there's work a-plenty, not lifting a hand. I allus wanted to bring up my chaps honest, never taking a thing unbelonging to them, never taking a grain they don't earn. It's folks forever setting bad examples that turns a child wrong."

Father had frowned. "If Samp ever got started digging—" he began, and then turned away, saying no more.

Fletch was listening behind the stove. "Now, I never tuck a thing unbelonging," he had said.

Father reached into the wood box for a soft splinter to whittle. Thin slivers curled under the blade of his knife until he held a yellow stalk bright with wooden leaves.

Fletch came from under the table to claim the splinter, taking it back for his play. We heard him blowing, shaking the leaves with the wind of his breath.

Father snapped the blade into its case. "Hit's a sight how good the mining business is getting," he said. "Big need for bunker coal up at the lakes, afar yonder. Jobs laying around loose for them with the notion to work."

Uncle Samp looked frightened. The veins on his cheeks burned full and red.

"Samp, if you want me to speak to Darb Sorrels, I will," Father said. "He's foreman at Number Two, and the best man to work for I ever had. I was raised up with Darb, and figure he'll take on any of my kin if I just say the word."

"I seed Darb Sorrels this morning," Fletch said under the table. "He's the biggest man ever was."

"I saw Jace Haggin," I said. "He's a witty, and wears three shirts."

Uncle Samp settled the front legs of his chair on the floor. He hooked his thumbs together, pulling one knuckle against the other. A muffled cough came out of his throat. He grunted. "I hain't been well lately," he said. "A horn o' Indian Doctor tonic I'm taking after every meal."

"I got Harl and Tibb Logan put on today," Father said. He weighed his words as he spoke. Mother glanced swiftly at him. Her mouth opened in dismay, for she knew suddenly that Father's cousins would come to live at our house again, making us fretful with their dark and stubborn ways.

"They were setting in wait for me at the driftmouth this morning," Father went on. "I spoke to Darb Sor-

rels for them. I said: 'Darb, here's some o' my kin. I'd
take it as a favor if you'd give them a little mite o'
something to do.' And by grabbies if he didn't put
them to snagging jackrock.''

Fletch raised his head above the table, holding the
shagged splinter aloft, and looking at Uncle Samp.
"Recollect the time Harl and Tibb cut yore mustache
strings off?" he asked.

Uncle Samp's face reddened. He tipped his mustache ends and sat up angrily. "I thought them two
were holed up at Mothercoal Mine for the winter," he
grumbled. "I heered somebody say it."

"Mothercoal is just a one-horse mine," Father said.
"Allus a-hiring and a-firing." Then his voice dropped,
holding the words low in the small of his throat. He
looked guiltily at Mother. "I reckon they'll be board-
ing here with us. Might be along hunting a bed tonight."

Mother's eyes hollowed. Her hands grew limp about
the dishrag. I tried to remember Harl and Tibb. I
thought of our four rooms, square and large, believing
them enough for us all, and I could not think why
Mother would want us to live lonesome and apart. I
thought of Harl and Tibb and Father sitting before the
fire on winter evenings, legs angled back from the
blaze, speaking after the way of miners. They would

brag a little, drawing back the corners of their mouths. "I loaded fourteen tons today if I shoveled one chunk." "I heered a little creak-creak, and by grabbies if a rock size of a washpot didn't come down afront o' me. Hit scared my gizzard, I tell you." "I set me a charge o' powder, lit the fuse too short, and got knocked flat as a tape." And Uncle Samp would speak from where he sat behind them, scornful of the mines, telling of what he had heard at the storehouse, and the others would listen as though a child had spoken.

Mother's lips began to tremble. She hung the dishrag on a peg and went hurriedly out of the room, her clothes rustling above the fry of the lamp wick. Father leaned forward in his chair, and then strode through the door, following Mother.

Euly turned from the window, where her hands had been cupped against the light. "I just saw a woman pass along, a-walking by herself," she said. "She might be the fortune-teller going somewheres in the night."

Uncle Samp's eyes lighted up. They opened round and wide. "Has she gone beyond sight?" he asked.

"Gone off down the road," Euly said.

"Coonie Todd, it might o' been," Uncle Samp said. "She's a widow woman, fair as a picture-piece. She goes a-traipsing all hours, selling broadsides with verses writ on them."

"What do them verses say?" I asked.

"They're writ about her man getting killed in the mines," Uncle Samp said. "I forget how the lines run, but they've got rhymy words on the ends. Hit's music not set to notes."

"Wisht I had me a broadside," I said.

"For any piece o' money," Uncle Samp said, "be it a penny or greenback, Coonie Todd'll shuck off one of them broadsides from a little deck she's got."

Euly turned from the window, blinking at the light. "If I had some money, I'd get my fortune told," she said, "a-knowing who I'll marry, dark or fair, and who'll be coming to my wedding."

"I know where they's a mess o' pennies," Fletch said, "but you'd better not touch 'em." He held the shaggy splinters high, pointing toward the mantelpiece in the front room. We recalled the four pennies he had found once. They were stacked inside the clock, behind the pendulum. "Was somebody to die, them's the pennies to put on their eyes," Fletch said.

Uncle Samp laughed, the web of veins ripening on his face. "Never takes more'n two," he said. "Two eyes, two pennies."

"Hush," Euly said, listening. We pricked our ears, hearing only the lamp wick's clucking for a moment. Then brogans shuffled outside, came nearer, and stopped. There was no sound of feet on the doorsteps. We waited, knowing it was Harl and Tibb, wondering how they moved so quietly. Suddenly Euly sprang back from the window, her face paling, fright catching in her throat. Fletch dropped the splinter, breaking off the shags. Uncle Samp jumped too, being as scared as the rest of us. Old Bartow skittered under the table. Two faces were pressed against the glass. Eyes looked in through a fog of breath; noses were tight against the pane, looking like wads of dough.

"Them two are born devils," Uncle Samp said.

I SAT with Father and Kell Haddix in the front room. A chunk of fire burned in the grate. Uncle Samp had gone to the storehouse. Mother was puny and lay on a bed in the far room. Euly and Fletch played quietly in the kitchen, it being too early for their sleeping time. We could hear bare feet whispering on the floor. They played frog-in-the-middle, making out there were a full dozen in the ring.

Kell Haddix's chin rose turtlewise out of his collar. His Adam's apple quivered; it strained in his neck. I looked, and it was like a granny hatchet's throat, swallowing clots of air. He lifted his arms, speaking. "They lit the Willardsborough smelter with a hundred dollar bill. A gold certificate. Aye, God, brother, I saw it burn." A pale wash of blue darkened in his eyes.

Father kicked at a finger of jackrock hanging from the grate basket. "Thirty years ago that was," he said, discounting. "The smelter's been falling a ruin twenty-five years nigh. No profit to dig ore in these hills. They lost money by the bushel measure."

A grim smile tightened Kell's lips. "That's what I'm talking. Money to burn. Hit's the same company owns this mine. They never missed that goldback out o' their left hind pocket. Money to burn, brother, and they're starting Monday to cut one day's work off a week. This time o' year the mining business ought to be juning."

"When I moved to Blackjack, I figured to work regular. But I've lived barebones long enough not to worry when my pay is cut down a grain."

Kell ran hands through his hair, scratching. His eyes burned in their sockets. "Got me worried. I've seen this thing happen here before. One day's work cut off, then two, three, four. The mines closed. Storehouse shelves bare, and no credit for victuals. The operators never stuck their faces in this hollow for eight months. I lived on here. You can't pack twelve children about like fodder. Twelve hungry chaps in my house and where the next poke o' soup beans was coming from unbeknownst. Folks moved away, God knows where. Whether they got work, I never heered. Fourteen families stayed, and there were times when all the meal barrels together couldn't o' furnished dustings enough for one pone o' bread. Twelve shikepokes in my house. Brother, that'll make a feller reckon."

"They tuck new men on here last week. Three o' my kin. I just says to Darb Sorrels: 'Looky here, Darb——' "

"Hit don't make sense, this cutting down and taking

on. Begod! They ought to hire Jace Haggin to do their business. A born witty could do well as been done. Oh, I want none o' my boys grubbing coal for a living. I'd ruther they'd starve in fresh air."

"Hain't nothing wrong with hard work, if they's enough of it."

Kell glanced at me, staring hard. "What, now, air you going to do with this scantling of a feller?" he asked. "Air you content to have him be slave to a pick?"

Father's gaze was steady upon the ceiling. "Why, I might make a check-weigh-man out of him."

I reached for the poker, stirring the fire. "I'm aiming to be a horse doctor," I said. "I am."

Father grinned.

"No bangtails in this valley," Kell said, "less you count the two blind mules Darb Sorrels has. Mine company used to pay their keep. Now Darb has to fork in his own pocket for their feed. Old now and ought to be put out o' misery. No more need for mules since they put wires in the mines."

"I'm aiming to cure all manner of beings, aside folks," I said.

"Oyez, oyez," Kell said. He drew his legs together. The bony knots of his knees were tight in the leg-bags of his breeches. He stood to go. "I'll kill my young 'uns off before I'll let them crawl inside a mine hole," he vowed. " 'Pon my word and honor." He moved toward the door, then paused. His shoulders sagged, his face became limp and resigned. "Oh, they'll be miners, I reckon. My chaps and yours'll be miners. Brought up in the camps they got no chance. No chance earthy." He opened the door, closing it softly behind him.

Mother heard Kell go and came into the room in a nightgown, my red coat about her shoulders. She sat close against the fire.

"Kell Haddix's a little touched," Father said. He tapped his head. "Up here."

"I hain't going to be a miner," I said. "I pine-blank hain't now."

Mother raised her eyes toward me in wonder.

"Darb Sorrels's a dog, if there ever was one," Harl said.

Harl and Tibb stood on the porch with Father, kicking heels of mud from their boots, scraping dirt crumbs from hob toes. It was Saturday, late in November, and they had come home from the mines with silver rattling in their pockets. I heard their feet grinding the floor and I came out from under the porch where I had been hunting rat holes.

"Darb allus has been square with me," Father said,

rolling his dynamite-cap pouch into a ball. "Little troubles are bounden to happen." He bent down, carving the mud away with the long blade of his knife.

"He's set us digging a vein not thick as a flitter," Tibb said, his mouth full of scorn. "Hit's eighty feet off the main tunnel, mixed with jackrock, and a feller's got to break his back to wedge in."

"Can't make brass, a-digging the vein," Harl said. "For a pretty I'd set a fuse and blow that trap."

"Stick and dig," Father said. "You're the last fellers tuck on, and they're already talking about cutting to a three-day week. Darb can't give a pick and choose. I say dig that coal, and don't start pulling any rusties." He shucked his boots off, taking them under his arm, and went inside in his socks.

I climbed the steps. Harl was shaking his feet like a cat come in out of the dew, his thin lips speaking against Darb Sorrels.

"I'll wash your boots for a penny," I said, "and shine them till they'll be nigh like a looking glass."

They cocked their heads, their eyes dark as chinquapins under the bills of mine caps. "What would you buy with such a bag o' money?" Tibb asked. They laughed, shaking their pockets, jingling their pay.

"I'd buy me a broadside off the peddle woman," I said. "I would, now."

Tibb reached up and caught hold of the porch joist. He was that tall. A grin wrinkled his mouth. "They dropped no pennies in my pay pocket," he said. "Get Samp to beg you a broadside. He hangs around that Todd woman every chance. This morning I saw him standing in the road middle talking to her, standing there with his brogans hitched with yarn strings."

Harl struck his hands together, laughing. "I nigh broke my neck stumbling over Samp's boots last night," he said. "I tuck me a blade and eased it through the eel-strings. They cut like butter."

"You oughten to do it," I said, feeling sorry for Uncle Samp. "Hit's not honest."

"I'd give a pretty to stick him and Darb Sorrels in that mine alley and set off a keg o' powder this side," Tibb said. "By grabs, I would."

They scrubbed their boots on the porch a bit more, clapped the carbide flame on their cap lamps, and went inside. The floor was dark where they stepped, marking their way over the scoured planking.

I pulled off my shoes as Father had done, tipping into the house. I set them on the front room hearth and looked at the clock on the mantelpiece. Fat smells of soup beans drifted from the kitchen, hanging among the beds. I stood on my toes, reaching into the clock, feeling behind the pendulum for the pennies kept there. I pulled them out, cupping them in my hand. There were four, worn and blackened, having no faces to speak of. "If'n I had me a penny—" I said aloud; and then I suddenly put them back, spying about to see no one was looking. I took my shoes and went into the kitchen. Father was warming by the stove. I stood behind his chair and looked over his shoulder, but I couldn't raise the courage to ask for a penny piece.

Harl and Tibb were already at the table. "The beans aren't nigh done yet," Mother warned, but they would not wait. They filled their plates from the boiling pot, whispering together as they ate. We heard Darb Sorrels's name spoken. Little wrinkles of anger dented their foreheads. Uncle Samp glanced up from the corner where he was making a hickory whistle for Fletch, a grain of uneasiness in his eyes.

Fletch heard too. He came and stood between Harl and Tibb, not being the least afraid. "I seed Darb Sorrels one time," he said. "I reckon he's the biggest man ever was."

Father chuckled in the deep of his throat. "The biggest man ever was come from Lower Mill Creek," he said, recollecting. "Died more'n thirty years ago, and he tuck a nine-foot coffin. Bates his name was, kin to the Bateses on Troublesome Creek. Baby Bates he was called. Stood seven feet six in his stocking feet."

Uncle Samp leaned against the wall. He was cutting a blow notch in the hickory whistle. "Abraham Lincoln was a big man," he said, "biggest feller I ever saw."

"You never saw Abe Lincoln," Father said.

"I never saw him in the flesh for truth," Uncle Samp said, "but I saw a statue o' him in Louisville once. It stood nine foot, if it stood air inch, and his head was big as a peck measure. Oh, he had a basket of a head to carry his brains in."

"That was just a statue, a-made big and stretched out," Father explained. "The man who hacked that rock picture carved him standing out on purpose."

Harl and Tibb held spoons in their fists, listening to Father and forgetting to eat. Father never batted an eye telling this tale. It was the bound truth.

"This Baby Bates, he wasn't just strung out tall," Father went on. "He was big according, head to toe. Three hundred and five he weighed, and not a grain o' fat he had. I saw him pick up Podock Jones once, rocking him in his arms like a baby. I like to died laughing, seeing Ol' Podock's beard waving up and down, and him looking like a born dwarf."

"By grabbies," Uncle Samp said, "I'm kin to the Bateses on Troublesome."

Harl's spoon clattered on his plate. "How much kin

air you to that queen bee who peddles ballad verses?" he asked. The black beads of his eyes were on Uncle Samp. "I see you two forever swapping talk."

Mother opened the stove door and took out the corn bread. She shook the pan to see if the pones were stuck. "I hear Coonie Todd's a good woman, and sets honor by her dead husband," she said. "Got a homeseat her pure own. That's more'n most folks can brag about."

"Her man's been dead three years," Harl said. "Three years buried and she hain't married another." He looked slyly at Uncle Samp. "I don't figure she'll be taking up with jist any ol' drone."

Uncle Samp knicked at the whistle. The vein patches were bright on his cheeks.

"That woman's the best song scribe ever was," I said. "Makes verses right out of her head."

"Reckon she'd make a rhyme about Darb Sorrels if something went bad wrong with him?" Tibb asked, stretching his neck to swallow.

"Now, looky here," Father warned. "Darb Sorrels could break a common man down like he was a shotgun. I'm agin starting trouble."

"I wouldn't be scared to tip him," Tibb said.

"Darb's been fair with me. Anything he'd name, I'd stand by."

"Feller can't make shoe leather digging that sorry

bone vein. Had my way, the roof o' that tunnel would be setting agin the ground."

Tibb looked suddenly at Harl. He spoke: "If that tunnel was closed—" then bit his words off. They whispered together again. They pushed their plates back and left the house.

Before the beans were fully done, I tiptoed into the front room and felt inside the clock. I took the rustiest penny—so black it looked like a button. "I'll put one back in its place the first chance," I thought. "I'm just a-borrowing." When I slipped it into Uncle Samp's hand he spied hard, at first not knowing what it was. I whispered in his ear, and he grinned. "I'll be seeing her tonight," he said. "I'll buy you a broadside for shore."

We sat down to eat. Our plates were filled with beans from the pot, the goblets poured full of butter-milk, the bread broken and crumbled. Fletch slipped crusts under the table for Old Bartow. Uncle Samp ate hurriedly, and set off on the dark road. We were alone in the house. There was none of Tibb's and Harl's tromping in muddy boots, or Uncle Samp's groans after a heavy meal.

"It's good to have a little peace," Mother said. "Hit's like Promised Land." The dread went out of her face. She glanced around the table. "You've every one got buttermilk mustaches," she said, laughing quietly. We wiped them off with the backs of our hands, and then we played a riddle game.

Euly had first go.

> As I went over London Bridge
> I met my sister Ann,
> I broke her neck and drank her blood
> And let her body stand.

"That hain't the way I heered it," I said.

> As I went through the guttery-gap
> I met my Uncle Davy,
> I cracked his skull and drank his blood
> And left his body aisy.

Fletch was anxious for his riddle, fearing we would know the answer.

> First green and then yaller,
> All guts and no tallow.

Euly and I smiled, knowing what this thing was, but we guessed wild.

"A parrot-bird?"

"A corncob?"

"Johnny-humpback?"

"Now, no," Fletch said.

Fletch got down from the table and crawled about,

blowing the whistle Uncle Samp had made for him.
"I'm an engine pulling sixteen coal gons," he said.
While Mother washed the dishes we played crackaloo,
pitching beans at a floor seam. Mother lifted her hands
out of the dishpan. They hung like dripping leaves.
Her face became grave, her eyes dulled. "Pity it can't
be like this every night of the world," she said. "Living
apart, having our own."

Father became thoughtful, cracking his knuckles
one by one. "I wonder what sort o' rusty Harl and
Tibb are up to?" he said.

Mother wakened me in the black of the morning,
standing over the bed with a lamp. I saw the fright in
her eyes, and her trembling hands. The glass chimney
shook inside its ring of brass thumbs. She told what
had happened to Harl and Tibb—the little she knew,
all not yet being known.

"Living or dead, there's no telling," Mother said. I
jumped out of bed, and into my breeches. I jumped
out thinking of Uncle Samp and the pennies. "Two
eyes, two pennies," he had said, and now both Harl
and Tibb might be stretched cold, and there would be
nothing to hold their eyelids down. I was good and
scared.

Uncle Samp's bed was empty, the covers thrown

back from the trough his heavy body made in the mattress. He and Father had hurried to the mine when the word first came. Harl and Tibb's bed hadn't been slept in, and I thought how they had been buried all these hours, deep underside the earth, with nobody knowing whether they still drew breath. A chill fiercer than the cold of the room crept under my shirt.

Drawing on my red coat, I went barefoot into the yard. The road was alive with folk shaken out of Sunday morning's sleep, trudging over frosty ruts toward the mines. Daylight grew on the ridge. A smoky coldness hung in the camp. Men had their hands almost to elbows in breeches pockets; women clasped fingers into balls against their breasts. Voices rang in the air, arguing. "Hit's like it was with Floyd Collins. Recollect? Buried in that sandstone cave, yonder in blue-grass country." "What, now, would them fellers be doing in a mine, middle o' the night, I ask you that?" "Them Logans hain't caught in that tunnel. I figger hit's jist a general fall, the ground a-settling down of its own accord."

Euly came and stood beside me, watching, sleep still in her face. Sid Pindler and Ab Stevall went by. They craned necks at our house as they passed. Three boys ran the road shouting. "Look," Euly said. "Yonder comes the fortune-telling woman." I picked her from the others. She came hobbling, her uncombed hair tucked beneath a coat collar; she was old, old, and the seams of her face were like gullied earth. Euly drew back, speaking under her breath. "Now, never do I want my fortune told, a-knowing everything coming, a-knowing when I'm going to die."

I shook, though not from cold. My teeth struck together. "I wouldn't want a ballad writ about folks gitting killed in the mines neither," I said. "I wouldn't now."

The sun-ball rose, yellow and heatless. The burning slag heap near the tipple wound its smoke straight as a pole into the sky. The chill drove us indoors, and we looked over the camp from our kitchen window, seeing the chimney pots were cold, the people all gone to the driftmouth. I begged to go. I cried a speck, but Mother wouldn't hear of it. "Wait," she said. "Your father said he'd send word." And while we waited she brought a cushaw from the back porch, and began to peel away the mellow skin. "Three pies I'm going to make," she said. "Harl and Tibb'll be starved when they get back."

Euly's chin quivered. "Never a bite they'll eat," she said mournfully. "Their mouths shet for good, their eyes with pennies atop." She crossed the room, and I knew suddenly where she was going. She went out

of the kitchen. I heard the clock door snap. I stood by
the window, as quiet as a deer mouse, scarcely drawing breath. She came back looking hard at me, knowing. She whispered to Fletch and they both looked,
eyes round with accusation.

When the cushaws were boiling Mother got a bag
of cracklings. She crisped a handful of rinds in the
stove. "Six pones o' fatty bread I'm going to make,"
she said. "Samp and your father and all the other fellers digging will be hungry. Nary a bite they've had
this living day." She started a pot of shucky beans
cooking; she opened a jar of wild plum pickles.

A granny woman came down from the driftmouth.
We saw her through the window, her breath blowing
a fog. We hurried into the yard to stop her at our gate.
"What have they larnt?" Mother asked.

The granny woman cleared her throat. "Nothing
for shore," she said. Her voice was thin like a fowl's.
"There's a chug o' rock fell down, but no sound beyond. Feller says he seed them go in the mine last night.
That's all they know—jist a feller says. Oh, never'd I
trust a man's sight Saturday after dark."

She moved on, grumbling in the crisp air, and we
heard a tramp of footsteps on the road. The miners
were going home. They came on by our house, blowing into their freezing hands. They huddled together

against the cold, speaking hoarsely amongst themselves. "Them two hain't there, and never was." "Aye, gonnies, gitting a feller up with a lie-tale in the dead o' Sunday morning. Hit's a sin."

Fruit Corbitt passed.

Morning wore away. We no longer waited at the window, no longer hoping, believing that Harl and Tibb were buried beyond finding. The shucky beans got done; the cushaw pies, yellow as janders, were shelved behind the stove.

Mother gave Fletch a pickled plum and his eating of the vinegary fruit set my teeth on edge. Hunger crawled inside of me; though, larger than any hunger, larger than anything, a knot of humiliation grew in my chest. It grew like a branching root. "If only I never tuck that penny piece," I kept saying to myself, dreading the time when Mother would know of it, being sure Fletch would tell, for he could not keep a secret. "If only I hadn't borrowed—" And I looked up. We all looked, startled. Darb Sorrels stood in the kitchen door, filling the space with huge shoulders and the greatness of his body. His head stuck inside the room, for the door was not tall enough.

"We've come on that pair o' rascals," he said, his words and laughter sudden as a thunderclap. "They blew up the tunnel betwixt them and the opening, closing that thin-vein place where I try out my new diggers. They set the charge wrong and trapped themselves proper."

"Are they hurt?" Mother asked anxiously.

"Not a scratch, and hollering to git out," Darb said. "Everybody give up and left except Samp and your man. They scrabbled and they dug, and now they's only a foot o' rock betwixt. Any minute they'll dig through. I tell you, that Samp is a man-mole. If I hadn't been letting men off instead o' taking on, I'd hired him on the spot." He glanced at the bean pot, the pies, the pickled plums. His lips slackened with hunger.

"When the digging's over," Mother said, "all of you come and eat. They'll be plenty."

"We will, now," Darb said gratefully. "I hain't et since last night. We would o' pretty nigh caved in if Coonie Todd hadn't set a bucket o' coffee biling for us at the driftmouth."

"Ask Coonie Todd to come too," Mother said. "Say she's welcome."

Darb turned to go, stooping under the doortop. He paused suddenly, his great head bent, listening. Boots tromped on the back porch; blunt steps passed into the far room. We waited. After a while two heads stuck through the kitchen door. Harl and Tibb stood there with clothes bundled under their arms, their mining gear hung over their shoulders. They looked at the table, then fearfully at Darb, and drew back. Mother opened her mouth, but no words came out. The door slammed, and they were gone.

"Looks to me you've lost two boarders and me two miners," Darb said. "But I'd been a-firing them anyhow. I got orders yesterday to let off a dozen men, and cut down another day's work."

Uncle Samp told us as we were sitting at the table. Coonie Todd sat beside him, weaving willowy fingers in her lap. "We're marrying soon's times get better, soon's work picks up," he said. His face reddened, the thread veins quickening on his cheeks.

"A feller who's got a doughbeater promised is square in luck," Darb said, his words booming with laughter.

"Nothing sorry as a bachelor feller," Father said, teasing. "A woman helps a man hang onto his money, and keeps him honest."

Euly and Fletch looked queerly at me. Fletch's chin was barely above the table. "Thar's one o' my pennies a-missing out of the clock," he said. "That hain't honest, now."

I felt shriveled and old. All I had eaten seemed a great knot inside of me. My spoon clattered to the floor.

Uncle Samp grinned. The ends of his blunt mustache pointed like 'fingers. His cheeks burned. He shoved a hand into a pocket and drew something out. It was a rusty penny. He spun it on the table. "I borrowed it to get a little chew o' tobacco," he said, "and I plumb forgot to spend it."

The bread was broken, the shucky beans passed, the pickle bowl lifted, hand to hand. Mother glanced at Father and Uncle Samp and Darb. She looked at Fletch and me. Her eyes were bright as a bird's. "All you fellers have buttermilk mustaches," she said.

FLETCH tiptoed through the kitchen and into the far room, closing the door between quietly. The latch barely clicked. He didn't see me behind the meat box. Only Old Bartow had found me there. I sat hidden, looking at the signs of the zodiac in the Indian Doctor Almanac. A man stood on a page with his belly covering off. Printed beasts and varmints circled about. "A feller going to be a doctor ought to know the insides of beings," I thought to myself.

I heard Fletch rummaging in the far room; I heard him stack one chair upon another, quiet as could be done. Uncle Samp was taking a nap on his bed and his muffled snoring was unbroken. Mother could not have heard where she rested in the front room. Fletch came out presently, passing on to the back porch. I peeped. He carried something in his fist. A hand was doubled tight against his chest. I stayed in my hiding place, looking at the odd picture-piece. Three meat pokes hung inside the printed man. I felt my own stomach, wondering if these things were there. Then I grew curious about Fletch and went to see why he stacked the chairs. He had reached to the mantel. A beeswax candle, a fox horn, and a pin pear lay upon the board.

Nothing was gone. Then I looked to where the dynamite pouch hung on a nail only Father could reach. Its leather mouth was pursed. "Couldn't have touched that," I thought and I went back to the meat box.

I turned the almanac pages. The moon and weather of all the year's days were there; moons with horns and faces like folk; weather flags flying red and white and black. An Indian doctor sat on the back cover. A feather grew on his head, and he held a giant bottle and a mullein leaf in his hands. I was thinking Mother ought to take this tonic for her sick spells when I heard a knocking, sharp, and steady, and near. Two rocks were being struck together. It was Fletch hammering I knew, hammering the thing he had carried in his fist. I went again into the far room, standing on a chair so as to see the mantel end to end. A dust track lay by the pin pear. I hadn't noticed it before. Fletch had balanced himself on one leg to reach the dynamite-cap pouch. I jumped to the floor and ran into the yard calling.

A rock thumped somewhere. I searched, sick with fear. I shouted.

Suddenly the earth shook. It was like a rifle-gun being fired into the ground at my feet. A cry came from under the house. I fell to my knees, looking beneath. Fletch crawled toward me, out of a smoke of dust. He came holding his right hand forward, a gore of blood dripping. Two fingers hung by skin threads.

I stayed on my knees, not moving, not being able to move. I heard Mother's agonized cry. I heard Uncle Samp's heavy tread. Running feet clattered the road. Neighbor women came, aprons flying. Fletch was caught up in arms. Voices were shrill, saying what to do.

"Spider webs quick, to stop the bleed."

"Lamp sut, I recommend."

"Get a handful o' fresh dirt. Dig under the doorsill. Dig down to the clean."

"Tie them fingers in place. They'll grow back."

Jace Haggin came, his face stark with sorrow. "Run and fotch Father from the mine," I begged. "Run and tell."

Jace turned to go. "I run fast," he said.

Fletch dozed on a bed, his right hand uncovered upon a pillow. Darb Sorrels leaned over him, studying the hand, and then went to sit before the fire with Uncle Samp, Kell Haddix, and Arlie Crouch. He threshed in the small chair. Jace Haggin squatted on the hearth, and Old Bartow meowed softly, for Jace was stroking his back. Kell was talking. "In July we got six days' work a week," he was saying. "Now come

February hit's down to three. If ever they's a time coal ought to sell hell-for-sartin, it's this month. Working three days now. What's hit going to be, come spring?" Kell and Arlie looked querulously at Darb, thinking he might know what was in store.

"Hit's ontelling," Darb said. "No use wearing your mind to rags a-worrying. I say take it as comes, fair or foul."

"Twelve chaps in my house—" Kell began. His Adam's apple leapt.

Father came into the room with a pan of water. He spoke quiet-like to Darb. "Reckon the fingers kin be saved?"

"Stands to reason they've got to come off," Darb said, his voice hoarse in trying to speak low.

"Might's well get it over then."

I looked at Fletch, and he was awake. He had heard. I spoke small into his ear. "Uncle Toll never cried when his finger was cut. Him just a baby too. Grandma said he never."

"I hain't scared," Fletch said. His lips were trembling.

"If'n you won't cry," I promised, "tomorrow I'll show you the pattern of a man's insides. I got a picture-piece shows."

"I hain't scared."

Father approached the bed, an opened pocket knife flat against his leg. The veins were swollen where he grasped the handle. I felt bound to see this thing happen. Fletch would want me to see. But I chilled with fear, and backed away.

It was over in an eye-bat. I saw nothing. Fletch made no sound.

Darb began to tear strips of flour sacking for bandage. "I tell you this chap's got nerve," he grinned. "I never saw the beat."

Jace and Kell went to look at the severed fingers. They lay on a trunk. Old Bartow sprang upon the trunk to look too. "A thing like that makes a feller reckon," Kell groaned.

"Little man," Darb said. "There's two gentle mules in my lot longing for riders. I'd be proud to have you and your brother come ride them sometime. Come when the notion strikes."

"Air them beasts still alive?" Kell asked. "I heered you was going to be rid——"

"Not yet," Darb answered.

Father whirled suddenly, glaring at Jace. "Put that there back on the trunk," he said. "Put back!"

"Born witty," Arlie Crouch blurted in disgust.

Fletch sat up in bed. His face was grave as an old man's. He held the bandaged hand before him. "How long hit's going to take growing me two fingers back?" he asked.

THE robins came back in February and black-headed cocks walked the camp yards. Robin hens grew fussy, pushing their pale breasts out as though shaping their nests already. The cold spells at Old Christmas and during the week Ruling Day fell were the only times I had need to put on my red woven coat. Miners cursed the warmth. They shook heads so fiercely cap lamps oft would go out. They eyed the sun-ball and quarreled. "Mines can't keep open long's folks don't burn fires." "Sweating in February, hit's agin nature." "Why, my babby-child has got a heat rash." They spoke of remembered winters, winters when ice choked the creeks, when timbers broke under its weight. They measured hands on hips, marking the snow's depth, swearing oaths as tokens of truth.

The mines cut down to two days' work. Houses emptied. Lanterns bobbed along the road at night as loaded wagons moved out of Blackjack. Idle men sat on the storehouse steps watching the shifts go into the pit, and they were there when the miners came out again. Uncertainty hung like slag smoke over the camp. Father grew quiet. He was worried about his job, and about Mother. Mother was ill, and often abed.

Her body had swollen until she could scarcely walk. She lay awake at night worrying over Grandma, for Uncle Jolly had written a letter saying she was sick. "Come for shore," Uncle Jolly had said. "Could I go see Ma," Mother kept saying, "hit would be a satisfaction."

I went barefooted through the camp, going where I was of a mind. Neither Mother nor Father scolded me. Fletch's hand was not yet healed and Father had commanded him to stay inside the yard. Euly kept indoors, cooking and bedmaking, and waiting upon Mother. The beds she made were lumpy as fodderstacks; she used a waste of grease cooking. I tramped the camp over. I saw what there was to see. I sat among tipple timbers listening to thunder of coal shaken into gons, and to the dolesome groan of conveyors on rusty cogs. I knew at last where the herb doctor and the fortune-telling woman lived. Under certain houses game roosters were kept hidden. I knew where. I knew the faces of men who pitted them in the birch draws above the camp.

I walked alone. Boys glanced oddly at me who had neither marbles nor spinny-tops. I gathered tobacco tags along the road, and around the company store, trading and swapping—three Old North States for a Bloodhound, five Bloodhounds for a horse-headed Dan

Patch. I did not go to Darb Sorrels's to ride the blind mules for a long time, though I ached to go. Fletch was jealous and had Father tell me to wait. He questioned me at night in Father's presence. On a day when I could wait no longer I gave him twenty-four Dan Patches. He vowed to keep my going a secret. He marked a cross upon the ground and spat upon it to swear.

I had in head going to Darb Sorrels's in early after-noon, but Mother was concerned about Uncle Samp. He had not slept in his bed for two nights. "Go look in-side the storehouse," Mother told me, "and if he's not there, ask Coonie Todd. Go to Coonie's house and ask." I went along the road to the store. Three men sitting on the steps leaned aside, letting me pass. I opened one of the double doors and spied in. Fruit Corbitt stood behind the counter wearing a coffee-sack apron, arms resting on empty shelves. Men sat about a cold stove. Three held roosters in their hands. They spat tobacco juice upon the brown belly of the stove, turning the fowls for all to see. Uncle Samp was not among them. I closed the door, and a voice came through it. "Hold on thar, boy." I opened it again. A finger was pointed at me. "Boy, I got a thing to ask you."

I walked midway the room. The man turned his

chair, facing me; he opened his mouth. He had a black tooth in his head. He pursed his lips to speak, but another spoke before him. A fellow leaning against the counter said: "Boy, who air you the daddy of?" The men by the stove batted their eyes. The corners of their mouths twisted.

"Brack Baldridge," I said.

Laughter rang like a sudden bell. Elbows were thrust against ribs. The men whooped. One began to cough with joy. Fruit Corbitt grinned. He thumped fists on the shelves.

The man with the black tooth did not laugh. His eyes were cold upon me. His upper lip drew thin. "Boy," he began, "I got a thing to ask you." The laughter hushed. The one who coughed sniffled and swallowed. "Your pap was amongst the last miners tuck on. And he's still a-working. Us fellers starved here during the shutdown. We stuck by. Now we hain't even got work, and your pap keeps drawing regular pay. Where does this stand-in come from? Air you kin to the operators?"

"Why'n't you ask Brack Baldridge?" Fruit Corbitt inquired.

A man stood up. He lifted a rooster in the bowl of his hands. The tip of the fowl's comb touched his chin. "My woman says one o' them Rosses used to court this boy's mammy," he said. "Luster Ross's got ownership in Blackjack Mine. I wouldn't put it beyond fact they got this boy on the payroll too."

Fruit wiped hands on his apron. "Don't plague the chap," he warned.

Words were hot in my throat. "I hain't never going to be a miner," I said.

The man with the rooster scoffed. "Hell shot a buck rabbit!" he said. "You can't git above your raising. Born in a camp and cut teeth on a tipple. Hit's like metal agin loadstone. Can't tear loose. Whate'er you're aiming to be, you'll end snagging jackrock."

I glanced hungrily at the door button.

The man leaning on the counter spoke: "I figger he ought to be a blue-grass lawyer. Sharp devils, the Baldridges. Why, two days ago that Samp traipsed out o' this camp, taking Coonie Todd with him. Said he was hunting work. Oh, he wouldn't hit a lick at a blacksnake. That widow woman'll woe the day."

"Them Baldridges——"

Fruit came from behind the counter. He had taken off his apron. "Let this chap be," he said angrily. His voice rattled in his chest. I looked toward the tall double doors. I turned and ran through them, almost tripping over the men on the steps. I kept running, drawing air deep into my lungs, and a voice was bold in my ears. "Whate'er you're aiming to be, you'll end snagging jackrock." It throbbed in my head like truth, and however swiftly I ran, it sped with me.

I ran all the way to Coonie Todd's homeplace. The doors were locked, the windows pegged. I knew then for sure Uncle Samp had gone away.

Jace Haggin sat atop a slate pile yon side of the tipple. He was whittling a pretty with a barlow jack. He saw me coming and hopped into the road, folding the knife, and beginning to stroke the knotched stick of a fly-jig. The wooden blade spun. It became a wheel. It hummed like a wasper.

"They's a rooster fight in the birch draw," he said. "I seed fellers set off. Us go."

I shook my head.

"I'll give you my fly-jigger," he said. He held it between his hands. The sleeves of his three shirts were unbuttoned, flaring at the wrists.

"I be not to go."

"I double-niggle dare you."

I shook my head, and walked on. I walked to the creek. The creek road went east and north toward Darb Sorrels's house, knuckled like a finger, pointing.

I stood by Darb's lot fence. No one seemed about. The lot was empty. A spout of water poured into an iron pot by the gate, spilling over the rusty lip. A sow grunted in a pen. Something champed teeth in a stable. A beast blew sleepily through its nose.

I horned my hands. "Mule. Mule. Muley."

The champing ceased.

"Mule-o."

A clothy rustle came near. It was behind me. I whirled. Darb Sorrels's wife was watching, her head deep in a splint bonnet.

"I come to ride the little mules," I said.

The woman peered out of the bonnet. "They've been tuck away."

"Gone?"

"Old, and blind, and puny. A sight o' feed it tuck, and times are getting hard. They'd a need to be put out o' misery."

"Gone?"

"Gone to dirt."

WE were eating supper and playing riddles around the far room hearth when Darb Sorrels came. We looked into his face and saw the worry there, and the dolesome cast of his eyes. A place was made for him by the fire, the rocking chair dragged forward. The rocker was the largest chair we owned. "Jist drapped in a minute," he said. He stood, holding hands to the fire. They were of a size to cover two men's faces. The nails were like scarifiers.

Darb refused to eat. Father and Mother pushed their plates aside. "Come to borrow a chunk o' fire?" Father asked. He was a grain uneasy. "Set and rest your bones. These chaps have got me stumped on a spelling-riddle. I need help."

"I'm bound to be a-going," Darb complained, but he sat down. He wedged into the rocking chair. It creaked under his great body. The rockers bent, hard drawn. The wooden arms were tight against his hips. He watched Fletch empty his plate, then eat leavings in Mother's. She had barely tasted the food. Fletch ate left-handed, his right thrust in a pocket. Old Bartow was licking Father's plate. Euly made a sign at Fletch, being ashamed of his manners.

"Little man," Darb said, "how's your paw healing?"

Fletch wiped his mouth with a sleeve. "Hit's well," he said. He got up and stood before Darb, though he did not draw the hand forth. He looked curiously at the great head leaning toward him. "I bet you can't spell 'swampstem,' " he said. "I bet."

"I can't for a fact," Darb said. "Sit on my lap and larn me."

"Now, no," Fletch replied, drawing away. He was ashamed to sit on folks' knees. He went instead to squat on the floor beside Old Bartow.

"My chaps are finicky," Father said. "Think they're grown before the scab peels off their nabels."

"I kin spell 'stovepipe,' " Darb said.

"How do them letters go?" Fletch asked.

"I hain't a-telling."

Darb's face darkened. "I ought to be a-going," he said. "Jist drapped by for a minute." But he did not rise. He swung the rocker, facing Father. The chair creaked bitterly, a round loosened in its peghole. "I been fotching an ax over the camp tonight."

Father sat very still. How small he looked beside Darb Sorrels.

"I've stopped a'ready at Crown Shepherd's, Reece Haggin's, and Tom Clearfield's," Darb went on. "I got six more places to call." His eyes searched the floor, unseeing. "On account o' Jace, hit's punished me most to fire Reece Haggin. A shame to turn a witty out to graze."

Mother listened as though she had not heard aright. Father had not told her of the lay-offs and the movings because of her illness and worry about Grandma.

"Next place I stop will be Kell Haddix's."

Father's cheeks grew ashen. He looked blue-pale and wizened, like a last year's dogtick stalk. "Reckon my time's come," he said.

Darb considered a moment, and shook his head. "Not quite yet," he said. "Not yet."

"Where air folks a-going?" Mother asked. Her voice was hollow, inquiring. Then suddenly she glanced at Father, her eyes large with hope. "Could we go back to Little Angus?" she said. "I'd be content. The first rented land ever I felt was belongen to me. And the baby is buried there."

Fletch spoke in the corner. "I recollect we lived on Little Angus. Recollect once they was three gnat balls flying in the yard. I shet my eyes and stuck my head inside one ball."

"Once a whirly wind come threshing a field," Euly recalled. "I ran to it. Hit spun me winding."

"I recollect the martins," I said. "I recollect——"

"That farm was sold for taxes," Father said impatiently. "Logging company bought, knocked walls out o' the house and set a sawmill inside."

Darb stood. "I'm bound to be going. Six doors I got to knock on before bedtime."

Fletch scuttled out of the corner. "You hain't told me how to spell 'stovepipe,' " he reminded.

Darb scratched into the thick of his hair. "Stove?" He seemed to have forgotten. "Ah, yes, 'stovepipe.' Stove to my rikkle, to my stickle, to my y, p, e, pipe."

Fletch's mouth opened at this spelling-riddle. He almost drew his right hand out of his pocket in wonder, but he thrust it back quickly.

Darb leaned an arm upon the mantelpiece. His head reached full to where Father's empty dynamite sack hung. "Son," he said, "I was born big and awkward. Never a chair large enough. Couldn't git my legs stretched proper under a dinner table. Against I was sixteen my feet stuck over bed footboards. Used to hunch my back, bend my knees a speck, trying to look like a human being. But them was fool notions. I be as I am. I got to be tuck that way. Well, now, I notice you're allus hiding that three-fingered hand in your pocket. I say, wear that hand like it was a war medal. Wear it proud." He turned to the door.

Father lifted both his hands, showing his leathery calluses. "Fear I'm going to lose all my hard-earnt badges," he said. He laughed. Laughter caught in his nose, in the top of his throat. It was a kind of cry.

UNCLE JOLLY drove a jolt wagon into our back yard on a windy March evening. We came out into the gathering dark with firelight falling behind us, and our shadows walked before like giants. Father spat into his carbide lamp, striking the flint on his palm. The flame spewed. We saw the wagon, and the weathered tarpaulin spread upon it. The mule sniffed the slag smoke; he blew anxiously through his nose, gritting teeth upon the bit. He rattled the harness with flank shivers. Uncle Jolly latched reins to the wheel brakes and jumped down. He squinted, lifting a hand to shed light from his eyes.

"This hain't a bird threshing," he said. "Don't try to blind a feller." His voice was dry with weariness. He glanced curiously at Mother. She was holding to Father's arm. He looked back upon the wagon, and we looked too. "I was a span coming," he said. "Hain't slept in three nights." He began to untie the tarpaulin, though he did not lift it. He untied it all around, and then turned upon us, angry because we did not understand. "Set two chairs in the house to hold the box," he said. We waited, huddled in the yellow light, not moving. He caught the tarpaulin and threw it over the jolt seat. A coffin box rested on the wagon bed. Mother drew back. She swayed, her knees bent, and she would have fallen had Father not caught her shoulder. He led her into the house and sent Euly after Nezzie Crouch. He came back to the wagon, whispering to Uncle Jolly. "Hit's getting near Alpha's time," he said. Uncle Jolly yawned. He shook himself. "You could tell from here to Jericho," he said.

The coffin box was carried into the front room and placed head and foot upon chairs before the cold hearth. Uncle Jolly opened the windows and swung the door ajar, saying the room must be kept cool as could be got. "Fotch spirits to put on Ma's face," he told Father. "I'm bound to rest a minute." He raised arms and yawned. A great weariness shook him, joggling his knees, jerking shoulders, flexing his mouth. His eyes watered. "Three eternal nights I been awake," he said.

Father brought a washpan, cloth, and soda jar. "Not a drap o' spirits in this house," he said. "Alpha says to use soda water. Hit's freshening."

Old Bartow stuck his head inside the door and meowed.

Uncle Jolly ran fingers along the coffin lid. The rio lamp shone full upon it from the mantel, and lamp fry and clock tick pitted the air. On the walnut sides of the box there was not a saw mark, not a grain bur. A good sawyer had built it. The box lid was raised an inch. I dreaded to look, though Fletch stood close and un-afraid, and I believed he did not know Grandma was inside. Uncle Jolly balanced the lid on the joints of his fingers. "Want these chaps to see now?" he asked.

"They'd better take out the mule," Father said. "He oughten to stand harnessed all night."

"He's not a court-day plug," Uncle Jolly warned. "He was bred at Mt. Sterling. Feed him ten ears."

"Corn hain't raised in a mine patch. We got not a cob. Loose him in the yard and I'll borrow feed, come morning."

Fletch tarried. He wanted to look under the lid. "If they's pennies needed," he told Uncle Jolly, "thar's some in the clock. I got me four a-saving."

When the mule was unharnessed we went into the house and saw Grandma. Her face was like a mold of tallow, quiet, and unbreathing. Mother sat beside the box, my red coat about her shoulders, combing Grand-ma's hair. Nezzie Crouch bent over her uneasily. The metal comb crackled among the gray strands. The hair was parted, reparted, strands divided between middle finger, forefinger, and thumb, and the comb caught back into it and drawn through. Two balls of hair were wound behind the crown of the head. A high comb was set into the balls, holding them poised and tight. Mother arose and her face was nearly as pale as Grandma's. She went back into the far room, and Nezzie Crouch followed.

I stayed awake during the long night. Fletch and Euly slept upon a pallet on the kitchen floor. Uncle Jolly unlaced his boots and stretched across the front-room bed, sleeping in all his clothes. He tossed and spoke words aloud. The chill of night air came through the open door. Father and I buttoned our pea jackets. I scrunched in a rocker, cold and wide awake, having no thought of sleep.

At eleven o'clock Nezzie Crouch came for Father, sending him abroad into the camp. She took the rio lamp away, leaving a squatty wall-burner. Flames leapt on the sorry wick. Shadow-moths beat wings against walls and ceiling. Old Bartow sat on the porch, and though I neither saw nor heard him, I knew he was there wrinkling his nose, sniffing. My eyes dwelt on Grandma. Now that we were alone I longed to speak a word to her, a word to endure, a word to go with her to the burying-ground. What word? I could not think. Father would be returning soon and I must hasten. My breath quickened. My throat seemed a stretched thong. I heard steps. I leaned out of my chair, my eyes straining toward the coffin box. "Grandma," I called. "Grandma."

Father came into the room. His teeth chattered. "They'll be a skim o' ice come morning," he said. I heard the back door open and close; I heard voices, and the chock of women's feet upon the floor. A fire was lighted in the kitchen stove. A tub of water was set to boil.

After midnight Uncle Jolly started on the bed. He jumped to his feet, stamping the floor. "Kill that robber cat!" he shouted. Old Bartow was sitting under the coffin box, his head lifted, his nose trembling. He had stolen in unbeknownst. He whirled, springing through the door, swift as a weasel. Uncle Jolly drew on his boots and did not sleep again. He sat on the brass-bound trunk rubbing his eyes, and began to talk. The wall lamp was burning steadier. The room seemed to wake.

"I fotched me a good mule all the way from Mt. Sterling," Uncle Jolly said, "and I've cleared new ground for planting. Grubbed roots middle o' winter, hit was so warm. Come spring, I'm going to put in an early crap."

"Spring's here a'ready," Father said. "Hit's been since Ruling Day."

"I saw green rashes yesterday," Uncle Jolly said, "but I never figure spring's in for shore till the basket oaks sprout buds. Never spring till a titmouse whistles lonesome."

Father slid hands into his breeches, seeking warmth. "You hain't told the burying plans," he reminded. "Alpha will want to know when she's able to be told."

"I'm doing what Ma said do," Uncle Jolly replied. "Taking her to Flat Creek graveyard." He seemed irked by Father's asking. He cocked his head, listening for the mule, and tried to peer through a window. "You know what?" he said. "When I come into Blackjack Holler I says to myself: 'Why's this camp so dolesome?' Dark was setting in nigh half the houses. Nobody on the road."

"Twenty-seven houses empty."

"Where on God's square earth did they go?"

"Somewheres, hunting work and bread."

Uncle Jolly eyed Father curiously. "You hain't been cut off?"

"I quit free-will."

"Be-grabs. Your woman called to straw, and it hard times."

"I tuck a notion."

Uncle Jolly shrugged. He lifted a hand toward me. "Never I'd be a raggedy-rump miner."

"Take a hook to your own weeds," Father said.

The squat lamp quarreled with a draft. A smoke thread wormed the chimney.

Uncle Jolly balled fists and thumped his knuckles. "Bracky," he said, "I've just about got my cats threshed. Ever hear o' that pretty girl I fit Les Honeycutt over? Tina Sawyers? I writ I'd be at her homeplace next Sunday, fotching Sim Mobberly and a license. Now you all can come and live with us on Lean Neck."

"I was born to dig coal," Father said. "Somewheres they's a mine working. Fires still burning the world over, and they got to be fed. All the hearthstones in North Americkee hain't gone cold. I been hearing of a new mine farther than the head o' Kentucky River, on yon side Pound Gap. Grundy, its name is." His eyes ran over the room, over the grooved timbers of the floor, the ceiling hanging high with no rafters, the bed, the clock, the smoking lamp. "Hit's a far piece to Grundy, three days' travel. Can't haul all our belongings. We'll sell and give away. We've got to begin over again. We've got to start from scratch."

"You hain't certain to get work."

"Nothing hain't shore this day and time."

"Hit's a blind chance."

"We'll make the bung fit the barrel."

"I say find out before setting off."

"We're moving from Blackjack to somewheres. Might's well be Grundy."

"Be-grabs if you folks hain't a pack o' Walking John Gays, allus a-going. Don't warm one spot o' ground for long."

An iron shoe smote a rock. The mule was walking the yard. We followed him with our ears. He nuzzled dry bluing weeds and the egg tree, and sounded a low bray of anxiety. He began to crib teeth on a fence plank.

Uncle Jolly spoke. "I aim to settle. I've got me a young mule, new ground cleared, and soon to have a doughbeater fair as ever drew breath. Bees to work my red apple trees, grapevines—" He paused. "And I got me a notion. Read in a magazine-book where a feller can raise and sell squabs. A passel o' pigeon boxes I'm going to build."

Father scoffed. "Hit's printed a feller can catch bull frogs and net butterflies for a living. All foolishness."

"I kin raise pigeons for a fancy."

"In jail and out, dinnymiting mill dams, forever plaguing Aus Coggins. I pity the woman you fool."

"Brackstone, you don't know square to the world's end. Aus Coggins allus blamed me. Allus I cussed and swore the contrary. Then I larnt who was punishing Aus."

"I'd swear it was you in a law-court."

"Ma cut Aus's fences, burnt his barns, and strowed salt over his land. His farm got briny as the salt sea."

Father glared at Uncle Jolly. "Hell's bangers!" he gasped. He knew it was the truth.

"Ma told on her dying bed, but I'd known a full year. Once I caught her hiding the wire cutters. And every time I went to Hardin Town she had me packing salt home. I never let on. I was that good tickled. Ma paid Aus his due, by juckers."

Someone in the kitchen closed the door between the two rooms. Feet passed quick and small over the floors. Father went to the door and stood for a while, his hand on the knob. But he did not go in. He came back to his chair, worried and restless, crossing and uncrossing his legs. "Alpha's so puny we can't go to the burying," he told Uncle Jolly. "Tell Luce and Toll we wanted to come."

"Why, Luce and Toll hain't going to be there," Uncle Jolly explained. "I'm doing pine-blank what Ma told me to do. On her dying bed she said to nail together a coffin box and get neighbor-women to make a shroud. I promised to take her straight to Flat Creek and bury her down alongside Father. 'Send nary a word to my chaps,' Ma said. 'They wouldn't come when I was low in health. No need they haste to see me dead. Of a summer's day when the craps are laid by you all can hold a funeralizing if you're of a mind. Get Brother Sim Mobberly to preach gospel at my grave.' "

"A body a-dying hain't in their right mind. You ought to sent word."

"I tuck a vow."

"You broke it a-coming by Blackjack."

"My mule needed rest."

The sleepless hours weighed upon my eyes. I dozed. On awaking, the blackness of the window was tempered with gray. Higher, along the ridgetops, light was growing. It was colder. My legs were bound with stiffness and my breath fogged. Father had tilted his chair, making talk, questioning. "What if this Sawyers girl says no?" he asked Uncle Jolly. A woolly mist curled out of his mouth.

"She's said yes a'ready. Jist never said when."

"Of a sudden you're in a mighty rush."

Uncle Jolly got up and stretched. He caught the muscles of his neck and shook himself full awake. He drew a great breath of air. "A man's the master," he said. "I writ that letter saying when." And then he turned toward Father, treading the floor to limber his knee joints. His mouth opened, rounding. A sly grin lifted his jaws. "You know what I done to that letter? In a magazine-book I read where a feller could buy sneeze powders. I fotched me some by mail. Well, now, I dusted that letter good and proper. I dusted it to a fare-you-well." Laughter rattled in his chest; it choked in his throat.

"Hush," Father said. He lifted a hand to an ear, catching for a sound through the walls. He had heard something. "Hush."

Uncle Jolly stumbled to the porch, smothering his joy. He clumped into the yard. Father stood again at the kitchen door, grasping the knob, waiting; then he went inside. I heard feet walking, walking. The kitchen fire was being shaken and replenished; the yeasty smell of morning bread hung on a windy draft. I closed my eyes, being near to sleep. I looked at Grandma in the dark of my head where I could see her living face. "Grandma," I spoke, "where have you gone?"

I waked, trembling with cold, and it was morning. The coffin box had been taken away. The chairs sat empty upon the hearth. I ran outside, and there were only wagon tracks to mark where death had come into our house and gone again. They were shriveled and dim under melting frost. I turned suddenly toward the house, listening. A baby was crying in the far room.